THE ROCKETS OF PYONGYANG

THE ROCKETS OF PYONGYANG

HANS HERGOT

WWW.HANSHERGOT.COM

THE ROCKETS OF PYONGYANG

Copyright © 2014 by Hans Hergot

Published by:
Bezzle Books
1492 Lake Murray Boulevard
Columbia, South Carolina 29212

The Rockets of Pyongyang, 1st print ed., 2014

ISBN 978-0-6922-9860-2

www.hanshergot.com

Table of Contents

True believers in an age of nihilism are as rare as unicorns. Only thing is, unicorns actually exist. There's the narwhal; and, if you squint, the rhinoceros.

- Danny Kim, Pyongyang, 2063

Chapter 1

Danny Kim walked up the stairs to his third floor flat in the High Castle Apartment Complex. The thick concrete building squatted on the Chinese side of the Taedong River, which stretched long and fat through the heart of Pyongyang.

Danny needed a drink bad, but not bad enough to use the elevator.

He preferred taking the stairs, didn't like enclosed spaces, the feeling of being trapped, the sense that he wasn't fully in control of his own destiny. Elevators were like that. Planes were like that too. He couldn't even think about rockets.

Beyond his quaint, communist-era apartment, rows of factories cranked out rocket parts, marring the once-pristine streets of the old capitol with pollution coughing smokestacks. The space race was being supplied from Danny's backyard. Capitalism had finally come to Pyongyang. Business was booming.

Danny passed the next landing, ignoring his reflection in the shiny steel door. He looked the same as any Korean, black hair, black eyes, black leather jacket and slacks, and a bottle of distilled rice wine in a brown paper bag.

He hated elevators. The slight jolt of stepping off an elevator reminded him of the pressure sensitive mines strewn all over the DMZ. The one that he'd stepped on wasn't like an elevator. There was no getting off in one piece. He blasted away from the earth, a rocket of one, the lower half of his leg separating from his body like a booster, falling back to the earth without him.

Thankfully, modern science could put humpty-dumpty together again, at least on the outside. They couldn't help it if the yolk got a little too permeable and started to bleed into the white. That's what alcohol was for. The bottle of soju he carried wouldn't last the night.

No sense taking the elevator, though. Like everything else in Pyongyang, the elevators were messy and only worked half the time. They smelled of piss ever since the Russian migrant workers moved into the neighborhood. On an elevator there was also the chance you might have to talk to somebody or do that awkward dance where they exit and you try to enter.

Worst of all was the passive aggressive notes taped to the elevator walls written by English expats living in the crumbling Communist-style concrete building. Dear apartment 12G, everyone knows your girlfriend loves you. Please keep it down? Dear Apartment 4F, house music is dead as you if you don't turn your bass down.

It was a wonder they'd ever defeated North Korea. Where had they gotten the courage to walk across the

DMZ and punch the fearsome North in its teeth? Not with the Ameritrash living in his complex.

It had taken real soldiers, real Americans, real Koreans and, of course, the *gyopos*, Korean-Americans like Danny, to subdue the warlike nation. And it had taken the industrial profiteers to finance the war.

Where else in the world except the internationally retarded North could you find a nation unburdened by carbon emission treaties?

The corporations hovered like vultures, descending as soon as the soldiers cleared the city, even faster than the Red Cross. Of course, the corporations had been forewarned about the invasion. They'd been prepared.

The industrial complex that had arisen from the ashes of war needed workers. It needed skilled technicians. It needed soldiers like Danny to run security. And it needed cheap labor like the poor Russian bastards it chewed up and spat out like so many potatoes in a vodka mash.

Ten years after the liberation, Pyongyang also attracted the sort of expats who thrived in chaotic environments. Those looking for an easy score, drugs or sex. Those looking to have an experience worth writing about.

Danny tried not to think about the tens of millions of people crammed into a city, each living in their own private bubble of the id. He closed the door to his apartment behind him.

On reflex, he toggled the lock and slipped the paper bag off the glass bottle.

Olchaengi, his personal assistant program, punched up the television screen in his living room. Footage of a jetliner burning on the tarmac at Sunan International Airport was all over the news.

Danny checked out the footage as he turned the cap on the soju, hearing the satisfying click of the seal breaking.

The attack on the commercial jet had all the earmarks of a nano-terrorist bombing. But that wasn't Danny Kim's business anymore. Not since Ye-Rin left him. That had always been more her type of thing anyway.

Danny took another drink.

He'd been stationed as head of security for one of the new space startups.

Domestic terrorism was somebody else's problem.

Danny cranked the door's manual locks by hand. He didn't trust home security to electronics. He put a chain-link lock in place last. Not that it would do much good, but it was something Danny thought every apartment should have. He was superstitious like that. He'd had the chain-link shipped from an antique dealer in the States. Good locks made for good neighbors, thought Danny.

That was the nice thing about an apartment in the city: he didn't have to worry about his neighbors. He didn't have to care. Danny tried not to stay up nights thinking about how his life was in the hands of a Russian who might pass out with a cigarette still in his mouth.

In reward for willful ignorance, he got as much anonymity as a crowded city could afford. Walking into his apartment was like walking into his own sealed off world, his own little piece of forever.

He glanced at the soju bottle, already half empty. He should have bought two.

Alone. That was how he liked it. The appearance of solitude was a beautiful lie, just like the world outside, a lie that could come crashing down from something as simple as a squirrel in a power converter or a knock at the door.

As if on cue, someone knocked at his door.

Danny couldn't believe it. He didn't want to answer. He'd just gotten home. If anyone really wanted to talk to him, well, they could put a note in the elevator.

The visitor actually rang the doorbell. Of course, that was a smart move on their part because the doorbell connected to a security camera. Danny couldn't help but look at the display on the wall. All this technology and his landlord still used black and white screens.

"Who is it, Olchaengi?" Danny asked his personal program.

Olchaengi replied directly into his ear in a sweet Korean accent, "It's your neighbor."

Danny wondered which neighbor might think Danny would possibly be interested in talking to them.

You can't help curiosity. And you can't help neighbors, not with a cup of sugar, not with a lost dog, not with a petition to protest the Committee on the Identification of Flagging Commitment to the Party, not if you wanted to keep that last little bit of anonymity, your apartment, your oasis.

Olchaengi pulled up the grainy black and white display. There in all its pixilated glory stood his next door neighbor, what's-his-face, looking so white that he nearly bleached out the display panel.

Danny undid the locks. He opened the door a few centimeters, the chain-link lock still barring entrance.

Centimeters. Danny shook his head. That was another thing about returning to Korea, land of his birth. They had him thinking in metric.

"What do you want?"

"It's Miles Birch. Your neighbor. Can I come in?"

"I don't know, Miles, I'm busy." Danny lifted the soju bottle and shook it for emphasis.

Miles glanced nervously down the hallway. Danny heard it too: the sound of the elevator opening and a slew of thick, Slavic accents spewing out into the hallway, drunk already and it was only six p.m.

Miles was right to look nervous. If those Reds caught a true-blue American like Miles out in the hallway alone, things were bound to get ugly. Not that Danny minded a mess, but he did mind when it happened on his doormat.

He slid off the chain lock and opened the door a little more. His arm still barred passage.

"What do you want, Miles?"

Miles ducked under his outstretched arm.

Some men were just like that, thought Danny, sliding in like rats without a backbone. Danny would have waited till the arm had been removed to enter. Or he would have broken the arm. Check that. He wouldn't be outside some dude's apartment, his castle, asking to come in.

Danny closed the door loudly as the Russians walked by, just to show that he wasn't afraid of them. The high-powered gun at his side ensured that he wasn't, though he'd have been just as happy to prove it in a fight, not a fair fight, mind you, since no fights were fair, least of all, fights with drunk Russians.

Inside the apartment, Miles paced the length of the empty dining room. No need for a table when you ate alone.

"Like I said, what do you want Miles?"

"I'm having some trouble." Miles pulled at the sleeves of his gray Izod-style jacket. The retro jacket matched the man's brown hair which looked as though it hadn't had a new style in twenty years. His thin mustache had gone gray at the edges, marking him as somewhere in middle age, though it was hard to tell with these desk-jockeys. The man might be twenty-five and a poor specimen of humanity.

Like all Korean men, Danny didn't look a day past his thirty-one years.

Danny gave Miles his strongest look of contempt. "Tell it at the Party's next community confessional."

"I, uh, I don't think they'd like to hear about it." Miles wrung his hands. He was standing in the foyer, looking as though his dog had been eaten, which, in Pyongyang, was a real thing. The man hadn't observed Danny's facial queues or perhaps didn't care.

Danny spoke up, "Why tell me? Why not tell your department head? Which area do you—?"

"You're the only one I know in the building. I'm sorry. I'm a theoretical mathematician, I—"

"I don't care," said Danny, holding up a hand. You couldn't talk to one of these science guys about what they did without getting a lecture. "Talk to the head of the math department at—which company are you here with?"

"SpaceSplore."

Danny's jaw clenched. He couldn't help the disgust that wracked his muscles every time he heard the names of the new start-ups in space travel. SpaceSplore. It sounded like a kids' show.

"Then talk to the head of your department or HR or whatever. That's what they're there for."

Not ten years earlier, Danny had been killing men, clearing out city blocks with a pulse rifle. Now he was standing in his apartment, talking to Miles Birch about human resources. The man had turned Danny's piece of heaven into his very definition of hell.

"They can't do anything for me." Miles walked into the living room and, without an invitation, seated himself at the table.

Danny was forced to follow Miles into the room in order to continue the conversation, which was a necessary evil if he ever wanted it to end. The view of the Taedong River stretched across the width of the patio windows. Across the river rose the new steel and glass skyscrapers of the various companies that now occupied Pyongyang.

"It's... I've been having some trouble with the Party."

Miles was talking about the North Korean Communist Party, which was still alive and well in Unified Korea thanks to democracy and freedom of religion.

The companies who ran the new and improved North Korea believed in democracy or at least the semblance of it. Maybe they hadn't realized that the northerners would vote en masse to retain their Communist system. Or maybe they didn't care since the companies themselves— the ones that moved in after the occupying forces with their vast amounts of capital—actually ran the city.

The companies loved freedom of religion too. The northerners had their own weird religion, *Juche*, all tied up with their mutant version of Communist propaganda. The northerners used their new-found religious freedom to stick right by *Juche*. They built a cathedral over the mausoleum of the dear leaders and continued corporate worship as though they were Baptists. Unlike Baptists, you could actually see the body of their savior Kim Il Sung.

"Dealing with the Party is simple," said Danny. "Go to a confessional. Fake a good cry about your supposed sin. Everything's forgiven. It's not like the old days. They won't send you to a gulag."

"That's just it. I think they might."

Danny waved him off. "Spit it out, Miles, whatever it was you came here to say." This wasn't a conversation he wanted to be having at all, nor did he want it to stretch even a second longer than it had to.

"People have begun to disappear. I think they, the Party, have been snatching people like me. First it was John... I don't remember his last name. He was—"

"That's not possible. The companies wouldn't allow it."

"I didn't believe it either. But then I consulted the oracle." Miles removed from the pocket of his gray blazer a set of black dice and a rumpled paperback.

"Get out."

"I just wanted to show you—"

"Out of my apartment. Now." Danny didn't have time to deal with crazy. Expats tended to arrive in Pyongyang in various stages of psychological decline. No one except the top dogs lured in by large amounts of cash and the delusional few trying to relive the glory days of NASA lived in Pyongyang by choice. The rest of the foreigners were the social rejects of their societies. For scientists, who tended toward social-awkwardness in the best of times, Pyongyang had become a sort of Mecca.

Danny went to the black and white terminal and checked the hallway. It was empty. Time to shuffle old Miles back into his little universe of rainbows and unicorns, where *yukhyo*, the Korean fortunetelling system, actually worked.

Dice rattled off of the glass coffee table in the living room, exactly where Danny's reheated dinner should have been.

"You see? It's the same," said Miles.

Moving back into the living room, Danny folded his arms.

"What part of 'leave' don't you understand?"

"But the hexagram—"

Danny emphasized each syllable. "I don't care."

"You should. I asked it who could help me. It said you." Miles pointed at Danny with both of his index fingers at once, his other fingers coiled around each other like a prayer.

Danny grabbed him by the elbow, putting just enough pressure on his nerve cluster to make Miles comply. The man scooped up the dice and his book with a free hand.

"It said if you don't help me, we both die!"

Danny had a grip on the door handle. He didn't turn it. Not yet. The man had interrupted Danny's afternoon. Danny was going to get his say before it was all over.

"You're a scientist. A mathematician. Why are you doing with this *sseulegigat-eun misin*? This superstitious crap?"

Miles didn't blink at the insult. "The *yukhyo* or *I Ching* is mathematics. Sixes, thirty-two, sixty-four. Just like computer programs. A *chomjaengi* in Seoul showed me the way to enlightenment through mathematical principles."

A *chomjaengi*, a Korean fortuneteller, probably one of the fakes in Seoul's Mairi district. The man must have conned Miles Birch. That explained how Miles had come by the *I Ching* and the dice. A certain kind of expat always came to Asia with the hope that they'd receive enlightenment, that an inscrutable sensei would take the naive foreigner under a wing like in a kung-fu movie and teach him the ancient wisdom of the East.

Danny shook his head. There was just no talking sense into some people. Danny turned the door handle. It was time for Miles Birch to go. Half a bottle of soju remained.

"You're a spy. I know you're a spy. And if they torture me, I'll spill the beans."

Danny pinched the man's elbow, adding pressure to the nerve cluster. Miles squirmed.

"What are you talking about Miles? I'm head of security for Next Wave."

"I know. I signed your clearance form, vouched for you, that you lived here."

"You did?"

"You asked me to."

"Why did you do that?"

"Because we're neighbors."

The elevator opened again. Danny could hear the door slide open. More Russians returning from work, drunk as usual. They were singing. It was a catchy tune: *necheevaw noi svyeta looshynyeto*. It could have been a folk song or an old commercial for all Danny knew. He closed his door.

For Miles, it meant a short reprieve before being cast into the growing dusk.

"Just out of curiosity, Miles. What makes you think I'm a spy?" Danny's eyebrows furrowed, doing his best impression of Bruce Lee looking hard.

"The oracle said."

"You know the *I Ching* is full of ambiguities? You shouldn't believe everything it—"

"And your father told me. The day he asked for a reading."

Danny's eyes narrowed even more. "When did you talk to my father, Miles?"

"When he was here visiting you on vacation last week. He was bored, being cooped up while you were at work. He visited me two or three times. The last time, he told me a secret, that you were a spy and that I should help keep an eye on you for him, to help keep you out of trouble."

"Miles," said Danny, frowning even more than usual. "My father is dead."

An explosion nearly knocked Danny off his feet. Smoke poured under the bottom of the door. The black and white monitor showed nothing but snow. Miles was bent over, clutching his head in his hands.

"What was that?" said Miles.

Danny could barely hear him over the ringing in his ears.

No need for Danny to ask his personal assistant Olchaengi for an analysis of the blast. That, Danny knew, was a breaching charge that just took out the door to his neighbor's apartment, Miles's apartment.

Danny knew this because of his military experience but also because he was, in fact, a spy.

Those Russians he'd heard in the hallway just moments earlier were either a Slavic hit squad or a team pretending to be Russian. Not that hard. Dress in tight jeans and black jackets and act very drunk. Danny was guessing the latter, considering the fluent North Korean dialect now filtering through the walls.

"Olcha, analyze those voices. Try to get a voice ID." Danny commanded his companion program.

He considered for the first time that evening whether Miles might be right. Not about the *I Ching*, but about the foreign scientists being nabbed. The operation next door had all the signs of a professional extraction team. If they were good, it wouldn't take them long to track Miles to his apartment. Danny didn't think that his sidearm, powerful as it was, could take on the kind of firepower those jokers would be packing.

With a look of regret, he abandoned the soju. Danny walked into the kitchenette and, reaching under the sink, retrieved an aluminum bottle. Danny popped the cap and clipped the bottle to the chain-link lock. He unlocked the door except for the old-school chain lock. Of course, he'd modified it. The middle link, if broken, would release a spark sufficient to blind and disrupt an intruder and, consequently, to ignite any flammable materials.

"What's in the bottle?" said Miles.

"Rocket fuel."

Miles's face blanched. And here Danny had thought it impossible for the man to look more white.

"We shouldn't be breathing that. You shouldn't have that."

Danny smashed the black and white door monitor, getting at the electronics underneath. He ripped the circuit board out, pocketed the attached microchip, and unceremoniously smashed the rest of the board under his heel.

"We won't be breathing it long, Miles," he said. "We're going for a swim."

"You just broke your monitor."

Danny led the mathematician toward the balcony that overlooked the Taedong River.

"There's a team in your apartment looking for you," said Danny. "You rang my doorbell activating the camera, recording your image. The chip had to go."

Miles nodded as though he'd been expecting an armed extraction team to come along. Maybe the oracle had told him.

"There's a walkway underneath the balcony. We need to jump away from the balcony about two meters in order to hit the river. And, remember, bullets only penetrate the first meter of water. Swim deep. But not too deep." While he talked, Danny emptied a stand next to the couch, removing drawers and stuffing his pockets with packet with documents, money, whatever he might need in a pinch. He spoke aloud to his program. "Olcha, activate turtle protocol. Wipe everything. Come back online at rally point Bravo."

"Where are we swimming?" Miles asked.

"Straight across. Unless they have a team on the other side, they'll never catch us. Not in rush-hour traffic."

"Ready?" Danny slid the door open. He went into the shallow patio and opened the outer sliding doors.

A sharp knock rattled the front door.

"Time to go, Miles." Danny pressed his insole into the patio railing and launched himself headfirst into the Taedong River. He missed the pathway below by a good meter. The instant shock of the cold water sent shivers down into his pants. Still, it was better to enter all at once than to slide in by degrees.

He sensed a splash beside him that he assumed was Miles. As Danny rose to the surface, a light erupted overhead.

Someone had forced their way into his apartment, igniting the rocket fuel. The resulting explosion blew a flame halfway across the Taedong. The concrete apartment acted like the top of a butane cigarette lighter, channeling a white hot flame. It was gone in an instant: whoof. That was the nice thing about that particular accelerant, thought Danny; not a trace left and it probably didn't even catch the couch on fire, meaning he hadn't just burned down the neighborhood. True, the impact might have killed the guy in the door and his crew in the hallway. But they'd invaded Danny's home, his castle. Anyone who did that deserved what they got.

Danny set off in a deliberate stroke toward the opposite bank of the Taedong, his cover blown and a scientific astrologer in tow. Definitely not the quiet night at home he'd been expecting.

Chapter 2

Danny set a slow pace across the river, yet the bookish Miles struggled to keep up. The Taedong River bent in a wide, lazy "S" through the center of downtown Pyongyang. The current wasn't strong, but the river was cold, fed as it was by waters flowing down from the Rangnim Mountains even further to the north.

Danny slowed enough so that he caught a glimpse of Miles in his peripheral vision with every stroke. He needed Miles to survive the swim in order to get information about who had blown up his apartment and about the man masquerading as Danny's father.

Being outed as a spy wasn't the worst thing that could happen to someone in Danny's position. It meant that direct lines of espionage were closed, but it opened up a whole new world of counterintelligence. Danny's new job was to hunt the spies that were hunting him, identify them, turn them, or kill them as circumstances dictated.

Danny pushed his left hand forward, slicing through the river. His right arm was cocked back ready to attack the water when he saw something that made him pause mid-stroke. A man was swimming after them. One of the team from the apartment job must have taken it into his stupid head to try to catch them on the river. It was supremely dumb. Danny was armed. All he had to do was reach the other shore and give the bastard his own personal reenactment of the Bay of Pigs, plugging him full of holes before he ever got out of the water.

Of course, their pursuer couldn't have known he was dealing spy of Danny's caliber. If the team had known who he was, no way would they have breached his door so casually. They thought they were dealing with a dumpy math geek and his unfortunate neighbor. The problem, Danny realized, was the enemy was somewhat correct. At the rate he was gaining, the man would easily overtake the dumpy math geek.

While the man tangled with Miles, Danny could make a clean getaway. But critical information might die with the doughy human calculator.

Danny sighed.

Taking a deep breath, Danny disappeared under the surface of the Taedong River.

He willed his body to sink a few meters. Having kept his shoes and clothing on during the swim helped combat his body's natural buoyancy. Danny came to a quiet, equilibious rest below the surface, waiting for the other swimmers to arrive.

Miles passed over him first. Danny could see the man's problem right away. His stroke was shallow and he was hardly using his legs at all. You'd think being pursued by a killer would've made him more energetic. Of course, it was possible that Miles was oblivious to the presence of the other swimmer, as he'd been oblivious to so many other things.

As Miles swam past, an object escaped his pocket, floating down toward Danny. One of the black dice turned end over end, rolling lines of light, lines of dark, lines of changes. His first instinct was to let it sink into the depths of the Taedong. Worse things had been lost to those waters.

Instead, he reached out, taking the die in his hand. A long, unbroken line stared back at him from the face of the die. A light line. An omen of change. He ignored it, placing the die in his back pocket and buttoning it up.

The pursuer was approaching.

Danny reached toward his ankle, removing a serrated combat knife. There would be no dramatic wrestling match in the water.

He slid up, silent as a shark. The man had no idea he was even there, floating parallel just beneath him. That's the problem with dark water, thought Danny: you never know what's just under the surface.

Danny arm moved slowly through the water, slitting the man's throat.

He scissor kicked to the side to avoid the death throes. When Danny surfaced, the man was floating in a growing pool of his own blood.

Next came the gristly part. Danny had to search the corpse. He knew there was no way a professional extraction team would carry any identification papers. But like any good spy, Danny was a little bit OCD.

He couldn't not look.

* * *

"You're bleeding."

"It's not my blood," said Danny as he pulled himself out of the cold river. His soggy slacks slapped against the insides of his legs as he strode purposefully toward the nearby walking trail that ran the length of the Taedong. Thankfully, no pedestrians were out enjoying an afternoon stroll. Pyongyang wasn't that kind of town. Not with all the foreigners from every nation spilling in to take advantage of the modern gold rush. Diversity in such close quarters did not make for better neighbors. It was like living inside a prison. The only people you trusted were those with the same skin color.

Unfortunately for Danny, born an orphan in Korea, raised in America, sides were hard to choose. *Gyopos* like Danny were "bananas"—yellow on the outside, white on the inside.

Danny overturned one of the trash receptacles. There was one for garbage, one for paper, and one for recycling. He turned the paper bin on its head, vomiting its contents onto the sidewalk: yesterday's news and a handful of bad lottery tickets. Danny wasn't trying to build a nest. He didn't need the paper. What he needed was underneath the recycling bin, which he'd set up as his own personal dead drop.

He put his hand into the can, pulling out a false bottom. In a few quick movements, he dumped a black duffel bag onto the sidewalk. For a drop like this to stay inconspicuous, he had to keep everything light. No heavy hardware. To reach his big guns, he'd have to play it smart. Danny punched a button on a piece of webbed plastic, tossing it into the air.

"Talk to me, Olchaengi." Danny commanded the machine to come online, channeling his companion program into the onboard computer.

Miles stroked his thin mustache. "Is that a drone?"

"Yeah. Everyone's got 'em these days." That was somewhat true. Having a personal drone fluttering over your shoulder had become something of a fashion accessory. It made walking the streets annoying. Humans had evolved for a millennium to avoid running into other humans. Stupid, low-flying UFOs? Not so much.

Danny slipped the pair of controller glasses over his eyes. On contact with his skin, they polarized instantly to match the glare and angle of the sun.

Immediately, a red triangle flashed in Danny's peripheral vision.

"Incoming fire." From an implant in his cheekbones, a vibration rattled his ears making Danny think he was hearing the happy-go-lucky voice of a Korean teenage girl. It was the default voice for Olchaengi, his companion program. He'd never bothered to change it. Her Konglish accent was heavy, very Korean-English.

Danny grabbed Miles by the shoulder, hustling him low to the ground behind the recycling bins just as the recycling container exploded. Leftover carbonated soda spewed into the air.

"Somebody's shooting at us from your apartment, Miles."

It was a stupid-hard shot for a sniper to take, especially with the wind coming off the mountains following the river. The distance wasn't bad though. It was one of the things Danny liked about the apartment. It gave him a clear shot onto the far shore and onto both the Okryu the Taedong bridges that connected the Chinese section of the city to the Korean-Western side. If the sniper sitting in Miles's apartment was any good, they were sitting ducks. Of course, if he'd been good, one of them would be dead already.

The warning sign in Danny's glasses shifted from a red triangle to a glowing red dot outlined with three red circles that pulsed in quick succession. He didn't need to hear Olchaengi tell him what was coming next.

"Somebody's painting us with a laser." Danny cursed. He'd hoped he wouldn't have to reveal himself so early. Once the attackers knew they were dealing with someone with his tech savvy, they'd likely change tactics. Ducking behind trashcans was a natural move for anyone being shot at. Not everybody knew how to circumvent a targeted drone strike.

Inside the red dot in his vision, a countdown began cycling from 9 toward the inevitable. Olchaengi counted it off in his ears.

Danny pulled a small plastic brick out of the duffel bag. He flipped a safety switch on the side, then toggled another button on the top. The countdown had fallen to 3...2...1. Behind them a building exploded.

Danny tossed a smoke grenade adding to the chaos. Miles was wiping debris out of his hair with both hands like a monkey. He had no clue what was going on and wasn't reacting particularly sanely, which was hardly unusual for someone who'd never come under fire.

Grabbing Miles by the elbow, Danny led him double-time toward the edge of the nearest building, another Communist monstrosity of reinforced concrete. His drone hovered silently behind them.

Danny heard the corner of the building pop. The sniper had nearly taken a piece out of Miles's shoulder with that shot.

Danny scanned the small street onto which they'd emerged. The red dot in his vision shifted to green before fading out. They were out of range, for now.

"Let me see the streets," said Danny, talking to Olcha. The heads-up display in his glasses brought up the traffic cameras in the nearby streets. He saw no sign on immediate pursuit.

Miles must have thought Danny was talking to him. "What?"

"One of your buddies over there called in a drone strike on us. Must want you dead real bad to drop a missile on us. Those things cost money. We're just lucky they didn't get chintzy and use the 50cal," said Danny. "Electronic magic tricks don't work on bullets."

Danny started walking toward a row of cars likely belonging to whoever worked in the shops. No one had come into the street to see what the explosion was all about. Most residents of Pyongyang were too smart for that. The nosy ones were already dead.

"I jammed their laser. Just a little trick truckers use to use to fool the speed traps back home. But now your pals know you're not traveling with a poker buddy."

Danny grabbed a helmet off of a motorcycle that he'd stashed for just such an occasion. He forced the helmet into Miles's hands.

"Put it on."

"I don't like motorcycles. Statistically speaking—"

The mathematician didn't know when to shut up. Danny cut him off. "We're not riding anywhere. Put the helmet on."

"Why?"

"Put it on. Please," added Danny, laying on the sarcasm. "They have a drone up there, probably more than one covering this area. They have facial recognition. They can count the number of hairs on your arm."

He took the helmet out of Miles's hands and put it forcefully onto his head. It was a tight fit but would do for now.

"Okay. Here's what we're going to do," said Danny.

"What about your face?"

"What?"

"What about your face?" said Miles. "Why don't you wear a helmet?"

Danny cocked his head to one side. "Because I'm Korean, Miles. Facial recognition doesn't work on us. We all look the same."

"Really?" Miles sounded so earnest under the helmet.

"That's racist, Miles." Danny grabbed a baseball cap out of his bag and pulled it down over his forehead. It bore a bright red "D," the emblem of his favorite team, the Doosan Bears, the K-league's perpetual underdogs.

"They don't know who I am yet, Miles. And if I have anything to say about it, they never will."

Danny grabbed the handles of the motorcycle and fired it up.

"I thought you said we weren't going for a ride."

"We aren't, Miles. I am. Like I said, here's what I want you to do. I want you to walk two blocks up and one block left. Do you understand?"

Miles shook his helmet in the affirmative.

"There's a small coffee shop on the corner, the YumYum Cafe. It has a lot of little nooks where people can read or whatever in private. You follow?" He didn't wait for a response. "Walk there, find a very private corner, and sit down. I'll be back for you in one-hour."

"You want me to walk there with the helmet on?"

"I want you to keep the helmet on the whole time. On the street, in the shop."

"Won't I look strange walking down the street in a helmet?"

"No stranger than you'll look if they put a 50cal through your head if they see your face."

"At the cafe, won't someone say something?"

"This is Pyongyang. You won't even be the strangest customer they've had this week." Danny revved the bike engine. "I'll see you in one hour. If not, ask your crystal ball what to do next." Danny handed Miles the die that he'd lost in the river.

Miles stared at it. A line of change stared back at him from the face of the die.

Before Miles could comment, Danny peeled out, cutting hard around the next corner. The tiny drone, piloted by Olchaengi, followed silently after him.

Chapter 3

Fading Communist propaganda, blue and red sunbeams pouring from the head of the dear leader, peeled off the sides of the buildings that Danny flew past on his bike. Televisions blared from open windows covered by steel bars.

The streets were lined with trash and narrow in a way that he'd only seen in Asia where the cities had not been built with cars in mind. Danny had seen the history films. Fifty years ago, a middle-class family in North Korea shared a used, Russian bike. Now the roads were packed with Samsung and Hyundai and even rich import cars like Chevrolet. That was why Danny was riding a bike, heading toward the Okryu Bridge that crossed over the Taedong River. Bikes were faster.

As he came out of the alleyways, Danny hit a wall of rush-hour traffic trying to get over the bridge. As in the days of the Kims—Jong Il, Jong Un, and his bastard son Jong Bae—only the rich could afford to live in Pyongyang proper. That much hadn't changed. The rest of the rubes, like Danny, commuted to work and slept among the dense, smoke-belching factories on the Chinese side of the river.

Danny weaved in and out of cars like a food delivery driver. Water from the river dripped off his synthetic clothing, ensuring he'd be dry before he reached the apartment.

While he drove, Danny handled intelligence and planned his next ten moves at the same time. Consolidation was the key to good spy work.

"Olcha, give me the view from Miles's helmet, audio and visual."

A small window appeared in the corner of his vision. He watched through Miles's visor as the man ambled down the street. He could hear the man's labored breathing as adrenaline gave way to stress. He could hear water squishing out of the man's sneakers.

"Mute the audio, Olcha."

Danny ripped a soggy wallet out of his black leather jacket pocket.

The team after Miles had not been professionals. The man he'd killed on the river had been carrying an ID. The wallet also contained a picture of two little girls. Danny regretted having to orphan them. But when it came to life versus death, it was just a business transaction.

He tossed the wallet keeping only the ID card. He held it up to his glasses while he sped down the white dotted line that separated the traffic lanes.

"Olcha, check this guy out. See what you can find."

"Affirmative, Danny." Olcha scanned the card and began a search.

He tossed the card in the street. He dug inside his pocket again. This was one of the things he hated about the spy business. Danny pulled out a severed thumb and pressed it against his left lens.

"Olcha, cross-reference the print." He tossed the thumb over his shoulder. It bounced off the side-mirror of a black Hyundai. He hoped the driver didn't get too curious. Olcha began running a parallel search.

"And, Olcha, open a secure line. Call Ye-Rin."

"No."

"What do you mean, no, you stupid program?"

"You specifically told me never to call her, Danny."

"It's an emergency."

"You said you'd say that."

Danny grimaced under his mask. The streetlights came on overhead, sending streaks of yellow across his visor in the growing dusk. It was too bad that programs had gotten so smart. But he was still the user.

"Override Gamma Six—"

"La-la-la, I'm not listening," Olcha sang to herself.

The Korean school girl thing was getting annoying.

"Olcha, you little pest—"

"You told me to ignore the override."

He must have been drunk when he gave that order. He didn't remember it at all. Then again, he always tried to call Ye-Rin when he was drunk, so it made sense that he would have put safety protocols into place to stop himself from dialing the number.

"Fine. Then send her a message."

Olchaengi was silent.

So, he hadn't blocked messages.

"Tell her, it's Danny. I need her to watch a white guy in a motorcycle helmet at the YumYum Cafe. And I need her to get there ASAP."

He watched as an orange message icon flew away from his field of vision. He pulled the handlebars to the left, narrowly avoiding a car that was changing lanes, thinking it could somehow get over the bridge sooner if it only picked the correct lane. There were no good lanes over the Okryu Bridge at this time of night. Not unless you were on a motorcycle.

A blue message icon appeared in his peripheral vision.

"Read it to me, Olcha."

"I can't, Danny."

"Another security protocol?" he asked his program.

"No, she told me not to. She wants you to read it yourself."

That sounded like Ye-Rin.

"Put it on the screen."

It was a single word: repent.

Typical Ye-Rin. He couldn't blame her. Their relationship had always been tumultuous.

"Olcha, respond with one word, lower case, help."

The message icon flew away. Danny concentrated on driving the bike. He was almost over the bridge and would soon have to cut right to get to his apartment complex. Danny hoped that somebody was still hanging around, so he could show them what he thought about being involuntarily evicted. Also, he needed to know who would be coming after him for having rescued Miles Birch.

A blue message icon popped up.

"Ye-Rin says you never asked for help before, Do-Song," chimed Olchaengi.

Great. She was using his Korean name.

"Tell her I'm asking now."

While he waited for her response, he checked on Miles in the corner of his vision. The man was just now sitting down at a table. He still had the helmet on.

"She says that this better not have anything to do with the airline bombing. She says she doesn't do that anymore."

"Geez, I know, Olcha. Tell her I know that. My house got hit. I just need her to babysit my neighbor till I can figure out whether he's involved in all of this."

Danny waited a heartbeat, which at nearly 120 kph seemed to pass incredibly slowly.

"She says okay."

Good. It was one less thing he'd have to worry about, at least till he got to the cafe and had the inevitable awkward conversation with his ex-girlfriend. Ye-Rin had been a spy, the kind who got information the old fashioned way. They had worked well together. Then she'd dropped off the grid. She'd got religion.

The age of belief had died long ago. Then came the ideologues, building a morality on foundations of shifting sands. All that was left now were the Danny Kims.

There'd always been something between him and Ye-Rin, but Danny hadn't been able to change for her. They could both lie convincingly. Why was it so hard to tell each other the truth? Danny shook his head.

"I know. Life's a bitch, right?" said Olchaengi.

"Stop scanning my brain, Olcha." The impish program must have been reading his biofeedback, sensing his doleful mood. The feature was useful. In a tight pinch, he might simply think "shoot" and Olcha would light up whatever poor bastard he was looking at without him every having to speak a word. But it was also a pain because the companion programs had been meant to interact with normal, dull people and to read their moods and respond with a sympathetic virtual shoulder to cry on or by piping in their favorite music. They hadn't been built for dealing with maudlin spies.

"Music," said Olchaengi. "Good call." She cued an up-tempo track from Jang Ki-Ha and the Faces, one of the first bands Danny discovered on returning to Korea as a teenager. The emo-hipster beat perfectly suited his mood, which was only natural, since Olcha was reading his mind.

Jang Ki-Ha's vocal riffs were weird and quirky. The same sort of thing that was about to happen back at Danny's apartment complex as he gunned the throttle of his bike only a block away.

"Olcha, give me infrared and get ready to watch my back."

The motorcycle skidded to a halt, it's front tire kissing the curb. Danny stepped off before the bike stopped moving, his gun in hand.

* * *

Danny hated elevators. They boxed you in, made you a sitting duck. Naturally, he took the stairs.

A man was standing at the base of the first floor staircase, leaning drunkenly against the railing. Russian clothes, but a tan, Korean face.

Danny shot him between the eyes as he turned to see who was approaching. Danny hoped he'd killed a lookout for the extraction team and not some poorly-dressed countryman.

Olcha had the man's face on file. Danny could look it up later and decide how guilty he should feel. Guilt was a luxury item that a spy could only afford in old age.

Olcha chimed with the results of the search on the man from the river.

"Give me audio only, Olcha." He didn't want his field of vision impaired.

As he went up the steps, Danny cleared each landing with an outstretched gun, checking carefully against Olcha's thermal imaging for signs of bodies approaching.

No one had shot at him yet. No posse came piling down the stairs. Danny decided that the poor slob below either hadn't been wired or that he'd never gotten a communication off.

If it was a real team, they'd know that their lookout's biomechanics had ceased to function and would draw the necessary conclusions. Or perhaps, instead, they were setting an ambush for whoever was coming up the stairs.

Olcha spoke to him, "The man from the river is Kim Tae-Kong, a low level thug with the Party. The thumbprint matched."

Rest in peace, Tae-Kong, thought Danny. He mounted the third flight of stairs. Thermal imaging showed a body leaning on the wall outside the stairwell.

Danny thought hard, *Go!*

"Gee, thanks," Olcha whispered into his ear.

She piloted the drone out into the hallway. Danny saw what she saw, a Korean thug in the stone-washed Levis that the Russians so prized.

Flash, thought Danny. He pictured a camera flash going off in his mind.

The thug approached Olchaengi, a look of curiosity on his face; his finger on the trigger of a full automatic.

A bright light erupted in the hallway from Olcha's small chassis. The man staggered, temporarily blinded. Danny holstered his gun and stepped into the hallway, his knife at the ready. Grabbing the man around the throat, he slid the knife between his ribs and into his lungs so that the man had no air to shout with. Drowning on land was a bad way to go. It was out of kindness that Danny snapped the man's neck on the way to the ground.

While this was happening, Danny's eyes never strayed from Olcha's point of view display. None of apartments opened. He saw no movement. No one seemed to have seen Olcha's supernova display.

The door to Danny's apartment was lying, bent nearly in half, against the railings in the hallway. A mangled body lay beneath it. A thick, brown streak ran from the doorway to the railing as though the would-be intruder had painted the floor with his blood.

The door to Miles's apartment had been blown in by the breaching charge. Danny stepped over the bloody trail and crouched to the ground outside Miles's apartment, painfully aware that, at this distance, the powerful rifle inside could easily put a slug through the reinforced concrete.

Yet, it didn't seem like the thugs inside had even the most rudimentary electronic surveillance. Maybe the low-level thugs employed by the Party didn't warrant any electronic surveillance support. To a spy like Danny, it was a senseless way to deploy an asset. But the Communists were not known for expending resources frivolously. Tales of Communist austerity going back to the Second World War were legendary.

Olcha's thermal imaging showed a man walking through the apartment, searching through what looked like a bookshelf. Heat still shone on the barrel of a sniper rifle sitting near the window. At least the man had had the good sense to shoot from inside the room, hiding the muzzle flash.

Danny watched in the corner of his vision as Miles waved a waitress away. So far, so good at the cafe. There was no sign yet of Ye-Rin. The booth Miles had chosen was particularly secluded.

He'd told her the truth. He wasn't calling about the airline bombing. That was no longer his beat. But he'd be lying to himself if he said that he wasn't looking forward to seeing Ye-Rin again.

First things first.

He whispered to Olcha, "I want you to go up and over the building. Come in through the window. I need a distraction."

"Anything special in mind?"

"You've got multiple options in your programming. Pick one."

"*Sweet-uh!*" Olcha's said in an excited Konglish accent.

The drone floated silently over the railing and into the sky. Danny watched her progress through the video display in his glasses, which were almost clear in appearance now that he was in the apartment complex and the sun had gone down. He caught a breathtaking view of the sparkling lights of Pyongyang across the river. The skyscrapers lit up the night like so many Christmas trees.

Danny recalled the images from the briefing before the invasion. Pyongyang had sat like a small candle in a darkened room. Hardly any electricity.

Now you could see the city from the moon. It was as bright as one of the squid boats that lured fish out of the depths of the Yellow Sea. Amazing what could be

accomplished in just ten years with an unlimited supply
of money and no bureaucracy to get in the way.

As Olcha dropped down, the view changed to the
interior of Miles's apartment. It looked like a mirror
image of Danny's place.

The intruder's eyes fixed on the fairly-like drone.
Danny guessed what was coming next. He coiled his
muscles, ready to act the second Olcha provided the
distraction.

* * *

Ye-Rin grabbed her purse and slipped out the back
of the prayer meeting. It was just like Do-Song "Danny"
Kim to call on a Wednesday night without regard for her
schedule. An *ajuma*, one of the older Korean women who
served at the church stood in the foyer. She gave Ye-
Rin a grave look. Ye-Rin bowed apologetically. The old
woman kept scowling, as though leaving the service early
showed insufficient faith. Or maybe she disapproved of
Ye-Rin's post-punk outfit, thick boots, pink plaid skirt,
and a blue biker jacket.

As a female spy who'd used her body to get the
information she needed on more than one occasion,
Ye-Rin was immune from the *ajuma's* grimace. She'd had
enough shame in her life. She was done with all that.
She'd found forgiveness. She'd found God.

The only thing she couldn't seem to get rid of from
her past was Danny Kim.

Descending several sets of stairs, Ye-Rin found
herself on a small street.

Her church had taken over an old office building so
that it could be located right in the middle of downtown.
Except for the blazing red neon cross above the door, she
could have been coming out of a dentist office.

Well, Danny's timing could have been worse, thought Ye-Rin. He could have called on a Sunday morning in the middle of service. And at least he was talking to her again. It had been a long time since he'd called. Olchaengi said he was even sober this time.

Ye-Rin keyed the ignition on a dark blue Vespa scooter. She popped on her helmet, pulling the half-visor over her eyes.

"Mal," she spoke to her companion program. She'd named it: *Malgeun Ggoom*. Sunny Dream. "Interface with Olchaengi. Find out what's going on with the man in the motorcycle helmet. And feed the coordinates for the YumYum Cafe into my navi."

She jerked the scooter off the quiet side street and into rush hour traffic. The heads up display on her helmet laid a map over the road, pointing her in the right direction. The navi showed that the YumYum Cafe was on her side of the city, right across the river from Danny's apartment, she noted. A countdown display showed her ETA: less than an hour. But that was counting traffic. She knew that, on her little Vespa, she could make it in half that time.

Unfortunately, other drivers had the same idea. She entered a swarm of motorbikes that buzzed like bees in and around the cars. Hitting a red light, thirty to forty scooters idled as close as they could to the oncoming traffic. A driver in a silver Daewoo gripped his steering wheel tight, angered by the audacity of the bikers. Scooters were the scourge of the road. The driver would have the last laugh though, when the harsh North Korean winter hit.

Anticipating the changing light, Ye-Rin tried to get a head start on the other bikes. Others had the same plan.

She found herself part of an impromptu motorcycle gang, speeding toward another collection of cars idling at the next intersection.

Her program, Mal, interrupted her concentration, "Connection established to Olchaengi. Patching you through to the man currently wearing Danny's motorcycle helmet. His name is Miles Birch. Olcha says that Danny is protecting Miles from some Party goons." Mal spoke through the earpieces in her helmet. He had a respectful, Korean male voice. Very eager to please. So unlike Danny.

"Got it, Mal," Ye-Rin said to her program. "Keep my mic patched through to the helmet but on mute, just in case I need to talk with Miles. Meanwhile, give me a composite of Miles; I need to know the man I'm watching."

Ye-Rin slowed her bike as she crept through the cars, trying to get nearer the light.

"Olcha, give me Danny's view as well."

"No can do, *Unnie*." said Olcha, using the honorific for an older sister. "You need Danny's authorization for that. And he's got his hands full right now."

"At least plug his location into my navi," said Ye-Rin. Then she had an idea. "What about your camera, Olcha? Are you flying drone surveillance for him?"

"Hmmm..." Olcha let Ye-Rin know she was thinking about it. Ye-Rin was betting that Danny hadn't considered the drone camera. Her suspicion was confirmed.

"It'll be our little secret, right, *Unnie*?"

"Of course, Olcha."

A second picture opened up in the corner of her vision. She saw a high angle of Danny taken from Olcha's view in the drone. He had his arm around a man's neck while his knife snaked into the man's back finding the exact right spot between the ribs. Ye-Rin had to admire his gristly efficiency.

"I hope Danny's not counting on me killing anybody, Olcha," she said. "He knows I don't do that anymore."

"We know," said Olcha. "*Unnie*, watch the road!"

The light had changed. A black Hyundai sedan picked that moment for a dramatic lane change, right in front of Ye-Rin. She slammed on her brakes, whipping the bike behind the back taillights. Immediately, the car behind her started crowding in. Bikes weren't given a lot of respect on the road. The only space they could occupy were the dotted white lines between lanes.

"I could've handled that," Mal said to Olcha.

"You two stop squabbling," said Ye-Rin. The car was almost kissing her back tire. Ye-Rin could see the female driver's intense look, as though getting three meters ahead in rush hour were worth more than Ye-Rin's life. "Mal, hack her engine."

"Finally, we're seeing some action again."

The car behind her went dead. The engine failed. The headlights dimmed.

Ye-Rin shot forward on her little Vespa as the idiot driver got slammed from behind by someone just as aggressively stupid. Ye-Rin never got the satisfaction of seeing the woman's face as it was obscured by an airbag.

"I thought you hated violence, *Unnie*?" Olcha chimed in.

Ye-Rin smiled. It did feel good to be back in the game. "I didn't do that. Her own recklessness caused that accident."

Ye-Rin had often used a similar maneuver when training in judo. Use your opponent's aggressiveness against them. Judo was, in the end, a very defensive sport. As a female, she'd been drawn to it.

From Olcha's camera, Ye-Rin saw the beautiful cityscape as the drone soared over the roof of Danny's apartment complex. Ye-Rin experienced "I can see my house" syndrome as the camera hit Revolution Avenue, the road she was currently on. One of those headlights lighting up the city might be her very own.

The view changed as Olcha descended to the apartment level. Ye-Rin saw what she assumed was the target: a man rifling through drawers, searching an apartment. But it wasn't Danny's. The layout was backwards.

"Whose apartment?" she asked.

"Miles's," replied Olcha. "Watch this, *Unnie*. Danny told me to make a distraction and to get creative!"

If Olcha were really a Korean schoolgirl, Ye-Rin imagined she would have been clapping and jumping up and down in delight.

But at the mention of Miles's name, Ye-Rin checked back in on the helmeted cafe customer. She saw something that she didn't like. That can't be good, she thought.

"What's wrong, *Nuna*?" said Mal, using the title that younger brothers applied to older sisters. He must have sensed her concern through her biofeedback.

"Ask Olcha if Danny is seeing what I'm seeing."

"She says they're both a little busy. She says Danny's in 'the zone.'"

Ye-Rin gunned he throttle. Miles was about to do something that would get him killed, and it was up to her to save him.

"Mal, I'm going to need more speed," said Ye-Rin.

"No way, the nitrous oxide? Awesome." He sounded like the typical male. "We've never done this before."

"That's because it's suicidal to put NOS on a Vespa in the first place."

"I told you. I ran the numbers," Mal argued.

"You made your point," said Ye-Rin. "And I installed the NOS. Now, stop talking and punch it. Oh, and jam the traffic lights—"

Ye-Rin's last word was lost in a squeal of tires and a sharp squeak of excitement from her lungs as the fragile scooter ripped down the dotted line between cars. She breathed deeply, willing her consciousness to expand in order to watch both the road and the small screen that showed Miles's point of view. She watched for the bullet that would soon be coming through his visor.

* * *

Miles tapped on the counter in a rhythmic succession, a mathematical sequence, counting with each finger-fall the same way an Oriental might have once used an abacus. Not that he had anything in particular that was worth counting. Miles counted in the same way people breathed—just to pass the time. He multiplied the count from his fingers against the number of corners in the room as he went from the corners of the ceiling to the corners of the floor to the corners of the partition, so many corners in this little coffee shop.

He thought about pulling out his black dice and asking some answers of the *yukhyo*, the system of Korean fortune telling. But it might seem a little odd. Even more odd than a man sitting, soaking wet, in a bright pink cafe wearing a motorcycle helmet. Danny hadn't mentioned that the coffee shop was one of the couple-cafes where young men tried to impress their girls with overpriced coffee. True, it was full of small nooks, and so many corners.

Miles had wondered if he should take a seat with a view of the door but had decided against it. Danny said he'd return in one hour. That was sixty minutes or sixty squared seconds. Miles began counting in sixes. He reached 234 before he had another idea. The bunch of toothpicks on the table might be used as yarrow sticks, which could also be used to create lines of dark or light in order to seek an answer of the *yukhyo* or *I Ching* as the Chinese called it. Miles picked up the stack of toothpicks and began to count them, amazed that he hadn't already.

The waitress returned with his order: a green tea smoothie. Of course, he couldn't drink it with his helmet on. And Danny had forbidden him to remove the helmet or even to speak. He'd had to point at the menu like a Neanderthal.

He overheard his waitress speaking to a colleague about the unique *sogaeting* or blind date. She must have thought he was waiting in an elaborate disguise for a partner. Miles's logical mind wondered what the point would be of wearing a helmet to a blind date, where the other party by their very nature wouldn't know what their date looked like.

He accepted the green tea smoothie and waited. The price of the drink was, of course, outrageous. The price covered not only the drink but the real estate of a prime seat at a popular wooing spot. Miles thought he should at least pay for his seat, even if he couldn't drink the green tea smoothie.

The diameter of the glass was about three inches. Miles measured it roughly with his index finger. Which meant the circumference was nine point four two four seven—his count was interrupted by a female voice speaking directly into his ear.

"Miles, this is Danny's friend, Ye-Rin. You can call me Erin if it's easier."

"Who is this?"

"Ye-Rin. I'm Danny's friend. Call me Erin. He asked me to look out for you."

"Where are you?"

"Doing about 140K per hour on Revolution Avenue, but that's not important," she said. "I need you to stand up and walk out the back door."

"No," said Miles. He placed the toothpicks carefully on the table. There weren't enough to create the randomness necessary to generate a *yukhyo* line. He started drumming on the table again, agitated. "Danny told me to wait here. Danny said don't leave. He told me not to talk and now I'm talking." Miles's voice dropped to a grating whisper. "I asked the oracle. It said I have to stay with Danny or we die. I didn't ask about you. I don't know you."

"Miles," she sounded so calm and soothing. Miles didn't know that Ye-Rin's personal program was piping subliminal, calming tones through the speakers in the helmet. He just knew that he instantly felt safer. He even stopped counting.

"Miles," she said, "you bought a drink with your card. The people who are looking for you will see that show up on the system and will know where you are."

Miles looked at the green tea smoothie and at the receipt. Nineteen ninety-nine. Expensive and a very strange looking number. Next to the number was his name and personal payment code.

"I didn't think—"

"No, you didn't Miles. We need to change plans," she said. "Danny is interviewing some bad men back at your apartment. We are linked together by navi and by our programs. Coming with me will be like being with Danny."

The woman paused. She spoke to someone else. "Olcha, show him Danny."

An image appeared in the lower corner of the motorcycle helmet. There stood Danny on the edge of a patio. It took Miles a moment to recognize his own apartment from the outside, looking in. Danny held a man by his ankles over the patio railing.

"Danny's busy, Miles. And bad things are about to start happening in the cafe if you don't leave."

"You want me to get up?" said Miles.

"And go out the back door," Ye-Rin completed the sentence. "Find a dumpster to stand behind. Pick up a cigarette butt and look like you're loitering, waiting for your girlfriend to get off work."

"I don't have a girlfriend," said Miles.

"Pretend you're waiting on me, then," said Ye-Rin. The speaker picked up the squeal of tires and an audible thud followed by a grunt.

"Are you—?"

"That was a close call," said Ye-Rin. "I'm risking my life for you. And you're risking your life every second you sit there. Now, get up."

Miles rose to his feet. The image of Danny holding the man over Miles's own balcony faded away. He didn't ask where it had gone. If Danny dropped the man, which it looked like he was about to do, Miles didn't want to see it. He had already seen the body floating in the river. Danny hadn't said how it had gotten there, but he couldn't have swum past a dead body without seeing it.

Miles got up and walked to the back of the cafe. There were three doors—a men's room and a ladies' room—and a door marked "staff." There was no back exit. Miles began to panic, shifting from foot to foot. He put his hands into his gray jacket, turning a black die over in his palm.

"There's no back exit," said Miles. He turned to look back into the restaurant. The waitress had come over to clear his table. He regretted leaving a full smoothie. It was so wasteful.

The sound of a thunderbolt struck the cafe. His visor polarized instantly, protecting his eyes from a flash of light.

When the visor cleared, he saw the waitress slumped over the table. Her right arm and shoulder were gone. Blood covered the pink walls of the cafe. His receipt and part of the wall were on fire. People were screaming.

"Miles. Miles!" Ye-Rin was shouting in his ear. "Go through the staff door. Get out the back. Olcha, paint a schematic on his visor. Make it so simple that a stick and a rock could read it."

A flashing red arrow appeared on his visor, orienting itself toward the staff door.

"Miles, go through the door."

"What was that?"

"It was a drone strike on the cafe. They correlated your payment to your table, scoped it with thermal imaging and deleted whoever they saw there. Crude but effective."

"It was my waitress."

"I know, Miles. You've got to move. There will be a team coming to double check."

"She was nice."

"I know this is a shock. I'm almost there. You'll be safe soon. But you have to go out the back. If the bad men come, I can't protect you. Go," the woman paused, "Three-two-one go!"

The countdown did it. Finally, a concept Miles could get behind. He pushed open the staff door. He didn't even need the swiveling red arrow to point the way forward. He simply followed the rest of the employees and kitchen staff out the back of the cafe and into the alley. The waitresses were hugging each other, crying. The cooks melted into the night. Probably not working legally, thought Miles, impressed with his own detective work. Danny wasn't the only one who could play the spy game.

A single headlight punched through the smoke that had gathered in the alley. He heard the revving of a two-stroke engine.

"Miles, it's me, Ye-Rin." The voice spoke into his ear. "I'm going to slow down. Slide on behind me."

"I don't— Motorcycles, statistically—"

"This isn't a motorcycle," she said. "It's a Vespa, an Italian scooter. And I'm a pretty good driver."

"Well—"

"I'll go slow. I promise."

Her bike was dark blue. It shone where the streetlights hit it. She was wearing a matching helmet with a half-visor. Ye-Rin was smiling at him. Not with her teeth though, which was good, because she might hit a bug and get it stuck in her mouth.

A blue leather jacket topped a pink and brown plaid skirt and a pair of leather riding boots. He stared at her legs.

When she came alongside him, she grabbed him by the arm, drawing him onto the bike. Miles threw his leg over the seat and gripped Ye-Rin tightly around the waist. It was weird, touching a girl like that. Miles wrapped his hands around her waist.

Ye-Rin shivered, "You're wet!"

"We swam across the river," said Miles.

Another voice spoke into his ear. She sounded like a school-girl. "You don't have to molest her. You could hold on to the bitch handle behind her, you know." It sounded like the girl was laughing about something.

"Who is that?" said Miles.

"That," said Ye-Rin, "is Olchaengi, Danny's companion program. Do you have one?"

"No," said Miles. He didn't even like relying on a calculator. He knew he'd get dependent and stupid like the other mathematicians in his office if he started relying on a companion program to do the heavy lifting for him.

"Well, they sometimes come with an attitude."

Miles could hear Ye-Rin in his ear and feel the vibration of her voice through the blue leather jacket. He marveled that a girl like that would even talk to him.

"Ooh, Miles, are you getting a crush?" said Olcha. "She's single you know."

Miles's grip relaxed as they idled toward the end of the alley.

"Stop reading his mind, Olcha. And you don't have to let go of me if you don't want to, Miles," said Ye-Rin. "Olcha, can't you see he's terrified of motorcycles?"

"I was trying to give him a distraction," said Olcha in a pouting voice.

"What do you mean reading my mind?" said Miles.

"Sensors in your helmet are picking up your brainwaves," said Ye-Rin. "Olcha was skimming your thoughts. Give him some privacy, Olcha."

"Humph!" Olcha pouted.

A pair of headlights belonging to a large SUV entered the alley in front of them. Ye-Rin slowed down.

Miles looked over his shoulder. Another pair of headlights entered the alley behind them.

"Miles," said Ye-Rin. "Sorry about this, but I'm going to have to break that promise about going slow. Hold on tight."

She gunned the engine, peeling out on the back tire as she turned a tight circle, heading back toward the cafe.

"Danny?" said Ye-Rin.

Miles heard yet another voice in his ear. This one was familiar at least. It was Danny, sounding calm and collected.

"I'm on my way."

Chapter 4

Danny held the man by his ankles over the Taedong River. The view was still magnificent as he looked out at the city at night. It was no wonder the magazines had started referring to Pyongyang as the next Singapore. There was an energy across the water that drew people to the city and a squalor on Danny's side of the river that drove people to want to make it to the other shore. Things always look greener on the other side, thought Danny.

He worked in the city. Correction, he had worked in the city till his cover had gotten blown less than an hour ago. The man dangling over the balcony was responsible.

Olcha had distracted the man while Danny entered the apartment. He had told her to choose her own method. She'd sung a popular K-Pop song. While her impromptu karaoke worked, Danny decided that he would be ordering the distractions very specifically in the future.

The only question in Danny's mind was whether to drop the man on the concrete pathway below or whether to give him a little swing and a sporting chance at a swim in the river. The man's buddies were already dead, one in the river and the others in the stairwells and balcony of the apartment. The leader of the failed extraction of Miles Birch was the only one of his crew left alive. Danny knew how the Party rewarded failures. It would be a kindness to drop him on the pavement.

Danny spoke slowly in Korean so the man could understand his accent, "Last chance, Comrade. Why were you after the mathematician?"

The man had a wicked-looking scar over his right eye. It might have even been intimidating were he not being held upside down.

"You're a dead man, you *gyopo* dog. You and your bourgeois masters can go to Hell. The proletariat will rise again uniting a true Korea into a glorifie...eyahh—"

The man never finished the sentence. He landed with a splash in the river.

Danny had heard enough propaganda speeches to last a lifetime, from both sides of the spectrum. After all, during his time in the Korean Army, Danny had been a member of KATUSA, the special battalion of Korean troops assigned as liaisons to the American military. Prior to the invasion of Pyongyang, he'd gotten the rah-rah speeches in English and in Korean.

These days, he passed Communist Party posters and meetings on a daily basis. Their street preachers, austere men and women standing on street corners preaching the gospel of Marx, were even more fundamentalist than Ye-Rin's Baptists.

"Olcha," he said, "I want you to follow the tracking device I planted in that man's shoe. I want to know where he's going and who he's meeting with. Try to get clean IDs from voice recognition. Also, if he comes within 100 meters of me, I want you to pop the device."

The resulting explosion would leave the man without a foot. It would be a sort of poetic justice for the way Danny had been treated by the Communist mine in the DMZ, though he doubted if the Party had enough invested in the man to justify leg reconstruction surgery.

Danny had been repaired courtesy of Uncle Sam and the war profiteers just in time for the block-by-block storming of Pyongyang. Since he was technically in the Korean military, he hadn't even gotten a purple heart like all his G.I. buddies. Well, at least his name wasn't on the memorial wall in Seoul either. Got to be thankful for the little things, thought Danny.

He walked over to Miles's black and white monitor. Aside from his mangled door and the matching corpse underneath, he saw nothing in the hallway.

Eventually the police would have to come. They were always slow to respond to calls on this side of the river. Tenants might have better luck calling the Communist Party for help. But in this case, the Party was already here.

He pried the monitor loose with his knife so he could get at the motherboard. He took the memory chip before trashing the electronics. Danny held it up against the light, looking to see whether the Party goons had messed with it, though there was precious little he could tell about the chip visually.

"Olcha, let me see your tail."

"Danny, that's naughty!" A quick image of the back of a school girl's uniform flitted across his glasses.

"Stop playing, Olcha, you know what I mean."

The drone flew in close, dropping down to shoulder level. Silver goo squirted out of a small hole in the rear of the flying craft. Gravity took hold of it, turning it into a short, sticky string. Danny grabbed the end of the string and stuck it onto the metal connectors on the memory chip. Olcha's goo had some amazing properties. The conductivity of the sticky substance made any device instantly readable by his personal program. Anything that couldn't be hacked wirelessly could still be infiltrated through its hardware thanks to Olcha's sticky tail.

"Olcha, we're looking for visits last week from a Korean-looking man old enough to be mistaken by Miles for my father. I want to see the man who cost me my career in Pyongyang."

"I got the data," said Olcha, retracting her tail. "Danny, Ye-Rin is sending you messages marked urgent. I didn't want to bother you while you were busy. I thought she could handle it, but now—"

Urgent? Why hadn't Olcha put them through already?

Danny checked the corner image that held the view from Miles's helmet camera. A scene of carnage in the YumYum Cafe greeted him. There was a dead, female body, and the walls were covered in blood and green gunk that might've been some kind of drink. Parts of the place were on fire. Miles was still moving. That was good news. From the angle of the camera, he appeared to be standing up, shaking his head in panic as he took in the scene.

"Olcha, patch me through to the audio. And I'm going to need a lift down to the street. Also, paint a target on anyone moving below. And I want the bike running before I hit the ground."

"Is that all?" said Olcha, laying on the sarcasm. "If you're in such a hurry why not let me try mannequin mode?"

Danny didn't respond to her sarcasm. And he wasn't about to turn his entire body over to her control. In mannequin mode, she could operate his body as though he were on remote control. Useful if you've lost consciousness or needed to perform a delicate maneuver. They'd practiced it in training, but Danny was not yet ready to be entirely out of control. Not just yet.

He grabbed the sniper rifle off of the apartment floor and tucked it under his arm, ready to fire from the hip. No sense wasting expensive hardware. Besides, if a goon popped out, at this distance, he wouldn't have to aim much. Danny raced onto the apartment balcony following Olcha. She flew over the railing and hovered a meter away. Danny vaulted the railing. He caught the drone with his left hand while keeping the rifle on the swivel under his right arm. He hated to think what the recoil would do if he had to fire it. His feet dangled toward the concrete, three floors below.

"Ugh, I hate it when you to this," Olcha complained.

The drone couldn't carry his full weight. They glided, jerking back and forth, toward the ground. Danny kept alert, looking for targets while he listened to Ye-Rin managing the situation with Miles. Immediately, his muscles relaxed. Danny felt good. His hand holding the drone almost slipped.

"Careful, there, Chief," said Olcha. "Mal is piping in subliminals, trying to keep Miles from freaking out."

"Smart."

"Mal has his moments, but he's not as good as me."

"Of course not, Olcha, not with the mods I gave you."

She had the bike engine running before he exited the apartment complex. Already the display in his glasses showed the quickest route back across the Okryu Bridge. Danny gunned the motor, peeling out for the second time that evening, as he headed—against traffic this time—to the other side of the Taedong River.

A pink blip on the map represented Ye-Rin. She was moving fast, way too fast for the little Vespa she drove. Maybe she'd gotten a new ride since they'd split. That had always been Ye-Rin's way of coping with one of their break-ups, except this one had been permanent, or so she said.

Miles was now in the alley, and Ye-Rin was pulling up beside him, managing somehow to get the scaredy-cat onto a motorcycle. Still the same Vespa.

She said she was a safe driver. Danny gave a short, barking laugh. She was Korean and a woman, and, while an expert at many things—Ye-Rin was anything but a safe driver.

Danny saw through Miles's helmet as Ye-Rin's bike was boxed into the alley by a pair of military-looking SUVs. That, plus the drone strikes, meant the Party— if that's who it was in the vehicles—was not messing around.

"Danny?" Ye-Rin was talking to him now. He started to gloat about her not being able to handle the situation by herself, but remembered she would never have been in that position were it not for his phone call.

"I'm on my way." Danny cranked the throttle on the bike.

Whoever was in the SUVs would not be pushovers like the fools sent to round up Miles. Olcha had already given him the readout on all the faces from the apartment extraction team, even the guy smashed under Danny's door. The OCD had compelled him to look at the body. He couldn't not look.

Except for the man that Danny had dropped into the river—scar face—the rest were local Party enforcers, real low-level types. Surprisingly, Olcha hadn't been able to dig up a file on the man with the scar over his eye.

As for the others, they were definitely not the sort to be driving around the city in military-grade SUVs following up on a drone strike that had just laid waste to a civilian café, which meant the Party had deployed its A-team.

Blasting the YumYum cafe was going to be a huge mess for the Party to clean up. They could keep things quiet, but not without the cooperation of other interested parties, namely the corporations and, of course, the other spy networks operating in the new rocket capitol of the world. The stunt at the YumYum was going to cost them, big time, which was all the more reason to figure out why the Party was hunting mild-mannered Miles Birch, math whiz and all around looney-toon.

"Ye-Rin, if they've called in a drone strike already, that means they have a bird in the area circling. If they put a tag on you, you're done."

"Don't you think I know that?" Ye-Rin was racing down the alley toward an oncoming SUV.

"Okay, what's the plan?" said Danny.

"You plan while I drive!"

Fair enough, thought Danny.

"Olcha, give me a high def flyover of the route ahead. Let's see what we can do to discourage pursuit."

* * *

Ye-Rin gunned the engine as hard as the Vespa would go without hitting the NOS. The little motor hadn't been built to handle two people at speed. Even her mods weren't going to make it possible for them to outrun the SUVs. Of course, they had to escape the trap before they could even think of running.

Mile's fat hands wrapped around her waist. She resisted the urge to shudder. As a spy she'd been called on to seduce men like Miles. But she'd been out of the game a long time. The close contact brought back a slew of unwelcome memories.

Ye-Rin concentrated on the danger at hand. The SUV facing them began to speed up. In her mirror, she saw the SUV behind her taking the same approach. They planned to crush her between the two armored vehicles. That was always a danger of driving a scooter on the roads of Pyongyang. Of course, there were things about her Vespa that not even the best SUV could reproduce. For one thing, it was much smaller.

"Mal, give me the schematics of the buildings."

Immediately, Ye-Rin began examining floor plans. She spotted what she was looking for.

"Feel like Chinese?" she asked rhetorically.

"I don't—" Miles response was cut short as the scooter skidded to a halt, facing a concrete wall at the back of a restaurant in the same block as the YumYum Cafe. The SUV was coming on fast, intent on sideswiping them.

"Open sesame!" Ye-Rin commanded.

The back door of the restaurant opened. Mal had hacked it. Ye-Rin opened the throttle, pulling through the door just as the SUV flew past her rear tire, taking the restaurant door off its hinges with an ear-curdling screech.

Ye-Rin negotiated her way through a very busy kitchen. The old Korean phrase "loud as a Chinese dumpling shop on fire" sprang to mind. Flames from the many woks shot into the air. A chef gestured at her with a large meat-cleaver.

Ye-Rin wrenched the big knife out of his hand and hurled it at the back door right as the first pursuer burst into the kitchen. He ducked aside. The shot he was about to take from his pistol went wide of the mark. The knife lodged in the door-frame.

There had been a time not long ago, thought Ye-Rin, when that cleaver would have sunk into his sternum. The enemy agent was lucky that Ye-Rin had changed her ways.

Her Vespa broke through the swinging doors into the dining room. Servers dived out of the way of the oncoming scooter and covered their heads at the sound of gunfire coming out of the kitchen.

It wasn't only the pursuer's pistol firing. A number of other guns added their throaty voices to the mix.

The Chinese kitchen staff was fighting back.

Ye-Rin realized that she must have inadvertently wandered into a restaurant run by the Chinese government or the Chinese mafia, which were practically the same thing. While this was a lucky break in terms of short term survival, it was somewhat problematic as to her long term prospects of living to a ripe old age.

Well, that was something Danny was going to have to work out. After all, he was the one who was still a spy and still had connections. Plus, he'd gotten her into this mess. He could explain to the Chinese warlords why their favorite restaurant had been shot all to pieces.

"Get the door, please," Ye-Rin shouted at the maitre d'.

The surprised man complied, opening an exit onto the sidewalk which Ye-Rin exploited.

She turned left, heading away from the YumYum Café. Thugs came piling out of the pink coffee shop with guns drawn.

At the same moment, the first SUV, having backed out of the alley, turned onto the street facing her.

Ye-Rin jumped the bike off the sidewalk. She heard an audible grunt behind her as the back wheel connected with the road. Miles hadn't been ready for the sudden bump. She was lucky he hadn't fallen off the back. Thank God that the bitch-handle behind him kept him in the seat, that and the tight grip he was maintaining around her waist.

She continued across the street, hopping onto a sidewalk and disappearing down a narrow pedestrian alley.

"So far, so good, Danny," she said, "How's your plan coming along?"

"Perfect so far," he said. She heard the sound of traffic all around him.

"Where are you?"

"I'm the handsome guy in the Doosan Bears hat waiting for you under the Okryu Bridge where it hits Revolution Avenue. Copy that?"

Mal centered the navigation screen in the center of her vision. She'd been too distracted to use it till now. A blue dot represented Danny.

"I see you," she said.

A concrete wall exploded over her head, sending down a shower of pebbles. Mal identified the source as an automatic weapon at the mouth of the alley behind them.

Ye-Rin scooted out into the next street, taking a hard turn as the pavement behind them got puckered by a hail of bullets.

"Bring the party my way," said Danny.

"Roger that," Ye-Rin twisted the throttle. "Mal, what do you think about the NOS?"

"With the extra weight? I don't know, *Nuna*. I'll run the numbers."

"We don't have the time, Mal."

The black SUV turned the corner behind them. It was so close that it had them in its headlights.

"Punch it, Mal."

The small scooter slipped ahead just before the SUV could ram it. There was a high-pitched keening in Ye-Rin's ears. It had nothing to do with the nitrous oxide.

"Shut up, Miles," she shouted. "I'm trying to drive."

The noise subsided to a series of whimpers.

Ye-Rin put the front wheel of the bike on the white dotted line in the middle of the street and concentrated on keeping it there. The rest would be up to Danny, God help him, she thought, and God help me not to kill him for getting me into this.

Not that it wasn't exciting. A small part of her, a very small part, actually missed this stuff.

God help her.

Chapter 5

Danny watched the wind ruffle Ye-Rin's plaid skirt as she blazed down the road, hunched over the handlebars of the blue Vespa. A jet of flame shot out the back, propelling the bike forward at an incredible speed. They raced in and out of streetlights, giving the whole scene a stop-motion feel.

Ye-Rin's hair, poking out from under the helmet, blew in the breeze. Miles clutched onto her back like a premature osteoporosis hump. Behind them, a black SUV bore down on the scooter.

Ye-Rin was smiling.

Danny saw all of this through the scope on the sniper rifle. Miles and Ye-Rin raced down an access road toward a ramp that led onto the Okryu Bridge. The Taedong River rolled lazily not twenty meters downhill.

The access ramps formed a looping clover leaf that circled around, under, and above the modern bridge. Lines of cars on the way home from work ran beneath

Danny, their headlights illuminating the bleak, urban landscape a milky yellow.

He was lying flat on his belly on a metal railing that ran under the bridge. It was a good spot to take a shot, especially if you didn't want the muzzle fire to be noticed by a drone overhead. Danny wondered why a drone hadn't rained hell-fire down on the little Vespa already. Maybe they trusted the SUV to bring Miles in alive. Or maybe with the SUV so close, they didn't want to risk a friendly fire incident. Not that the Party had ever shown much concern over killing a few of its own to get the job done.

The SUV was just a meter away from the scooter. Danny inhaled, waiting for the vehicle to come in range. He had to time it just right: close enough that he had a safe shot over Ye-Rin's head, but far enough that the SUV didn't get to the bike before he took his shot.

Danny exhaled slowly and gently squeezed the trigger down to the breaking point. It wasn't an orthodox way to shoot, but Danny tended to hit what he aimed at, thus making his technique a moot point. Olchaengi's drone sat next to the rifle. Her sticky tail probed the internal circuits of the gun, giving Danny access to what was otherwise a genetically coded trigger.

She peppered his field of vision with information on the wind speed and distance to target. She calculated the vehicles' speeds and translated that into a little red bull's-eye inside the scope of the gun.

"Clear it off, Olcha," said Danny. "If there's going to be user error, it's going to be mine."

He was shooting near someone who, up until a few months ago, had been the center of his world. Getting over their breakup had been hard enough. He didn't want to think what it would be like to have to mourn her death, especially coming from the barrel of his own rifle.

What was it people said about breakups? It's like losing a loved one, but you still have to see them, like a zombie, completely changed—so familiar; yet so completely unknown.

Olchaengi retreated into the drone, even dropping the visual feed from Miles's helmet. She had long since dropped the audio. The man was a whiner.

Danny took careful aim and fired.

The bullet put a crack in the windshield of the SUV but didn't penetrate the glass.

The thing must be heavily armored, thought Danny. The SUV slowed down, giving Ye-Rin and Miles a precious few-second lead.

Danny fired again, pulling off a shot that would rival Robin Hood. Danny scored a direct hit in the exact same spot. The glass fractured but did not break.

He took a shot at the front tire only to gouge the pavement. The SUV rolled over the hole.

As the scooter and the SUV neared the bridge, Danny laid down a barrage of rapid fire on the front window, right in front of the driver. He might not be able to get at the guy, but only someone with nerves of steel could drive through a turkey shoot without losing his cool.

The SUV swerved, but never lost track of the scooter. The access road that Ye-Rin was racing down was lined with parked cars as was common on every out-of-the-way street in the city.

Ye-Rin gave Danny a thumbs-up as she whipped under the bridge. He was too busy to respond.

Danny dusted the driver's side window one more time with the sniper rifle. As the van came under the bridge, Danny signaled Olcha.

"Now, Olcha."

One of the parked cars exploded. The flames rose nearly high enough to cook Danny. But he'd set the charge well. The exploding car punched away from the concrete barricade beside which it was parked, slamming into the side of the SUV.

The SUV was knocked off the road. It teetered over the edge of a small incline before rolling down onto the walkway that lined the Taedong. Rather than coming to a halt on the concrete path, the SUV continued to roll into the river.

"Good job, Olcha," Danny congratulated the little program on her expert calculations. The charge he'd been carrying in his bag had been whittled away to just the right size to achieve maximum propulsion for the parked car. He still had enough of the lightweight explosive left to do some more damage should the need arise.

Packing up the rifle, Danny slid down a caged ladder to the ground below. Olcha was in the air again, tracking his every move. Ye-Rin had come to a halt under the bridge. Smart girl.

Smoke billowed out from under the Okryu Bridge lending a certain degree of ambiguity to the scene should anyone be watching from the comfortable distance of a drone camera.

Ye-Rin pulled up next to Danny.

"We're going to have to ditch your bike," he said.

"But I got it after we broke up, that one time. Or was it the other? I forget. Anyway, it has sentimental value," she said. "It reminds me that I never have to see you again for as long as you live."

"You two broke up?" said Miles.

"Not now." Danny gave Miles a withering look, though between the tinted visor on the helmet and Danny's own glasses, which were still dealing with a burning car under the bridge, the look might have been difficult for Miles to see. Not that the man could read social cues in the first place.

"We need to change our profile. They'll be looking for your Vespa. We have to ditch it, steal a car."

"So we can get boxed in with all the traffic up there? We'd be sitting ducks."

"We can go against traffic into the city. I've got a safe house there." Danny crossed his arms. One minute together and they were already bickering like a married couple—not the kind that sat together in silence in a restaurant with nothing to say between them, but like the kind of married people who threw the wedding china at each other.

"Your love nest? No thanks."

Danny remembered that Ye-Rin had been there before, in another capacity, before they broke up and before she found Jesus. He had to reframe the debate.

"What do you suggest?" said Danny, "Remember the clock is ticking."

As he spoke, Danny walked to the nearest car and placed Olcha's sticky tail onto the front access panel. The door popped open.

"For starters, you can drop me off at church."

"Get in, Miles," said Danny, as he slid into the driver's seat.

Ye-Rin grabbed the saddlebags off the scooter before rolling it toward the grassy hill that led down to the Taedong River. Danny could see that parting with the bike was causing her pain. She pushed it over the edge and watched as it rolled down the hill and sank in the cold water under the bridge.

After all this blew over, thought Danny, he was going to owe her a new bike.

Miles took a place in the back seat. Ye-Rin got in beside Danny.

He eased the black sedan up the onramp, merging with traffic on the bridge.

The silence inside the car was in direct contrast to the noisy traffic on the Okryu Bridge. Though there were relatively few cars heading in their direction compared to the other side of the road, horns blared and were echoed by tremolo blasts from the motorcycles that wove among the automobiles.

Danny merged onto Revolution Avenue, retracing the route Ye-Rin had taken to get to the YumYum Cafe. Ye-Rin sat next to him with her arms and legs folded.

Finally, Danny broke the ice. "You have to stay with us."

"Umm," said Ye-Rin, "I think I've already proven that I can leave you where and when I want."

This wasn't how Danny wanted their first conversation to go. He hadn't meant to sound like he was ordering her around.

"It's not safe. They had to have gotten the tag number on your Vespa."

"Good thing I traded with a bike down the street."

Danny would have done the same thing. The thing to do when trading license plates was to find a new set of wheels, one where they hadn't memorized their plates yet.

"I thought Christians didn't steal," said Danny. "Or did you offer him something else?"

The question was mean and petty, and Danny immediately regretted it.

Ye-Rin didn't bristle. "I asked him for it. I'm not that girl anymore. I don't hook or kill or ride around in stolen vehicles, Danny."

That was the thing with most moralists, Danny realized. Their ethics operated on levels of scale. Telling a white lie was all right while telling a big lie was a mortal sin, like breaking a few hundred small traffic laws as Ye-Rin had just done versus stealing a license plate. Her driving that night could have gotten somebody killed. Meanwhile, stealing the sedan wouldn't hurt anyone. Even borrowing a license plate wasn't exactly harmless. Danny wouldn't want to be Ye-Rin's neighbor if the Party paid him a visit. He didn't bother to explain any of this to Ye-Rin. She had a way of turning his arguments back on him.

"Suit yourself," said Danny. "We'll take you to your church. Mal, punch it into the car's navi if you don't mind."

"I'm sorry, Danny," said Mal, "but—"

"But you don't get to order me or my program around anymore."

"Fine. Olcha, take us to the nearest pet shop. I'm sure Ye-Rin's church will be near a place where they can lay their hands on some snakes."

"First Baptist, Pyongyang, please, Olcha." Ye-Rin gave the directions in a pleasant voice, one that said that she wasn't going to rise to the bait.

"Right away, *Unnie*!" Unlike Mal, Olcha wasn't the least bit hesitant to do Ye-Rin's bidding. Then again, the two had always formed something of a conspiracy against him.

"Can I take my helmet off yet?"

Danny had nearly forgotten about Miles in the backseat.

"No!" he and Ye-Rin both said in unison.

Danny explained, looking back at Miles, "They're still going to be scanning faces, Miles. We— or I have to get you someplace safe, someplace out of the way before you take the helmet off." Danny touched the dashboard of the car, saying, "It's also good if you don't talk too much. They'll be looking for your voice print too. They can access a car's sound system and listen to whatever the passengers are talking about. With so many cars, there's not that much risk. But—"

"The statistics are low, very low," Miles added.

"Exactly, but not nil. So we need to take it easy till we can find out who's after you and what they want."

Miles tapped his fingers across his knees in what looked like a sort of mantra. "I told you. The Party wants me."

"Yeah, but why are they picking up scientists like you? Why not just hire their own?"

"Oh, they're not picking up scientists."

"I thought you said, back at the apartment, that they were after guys like you. That one of your buddies, Jimmy or something, got nabbed."

"Yes," said Miles. Then he gave a little giggle. Thankfully it was muffled by the visor. "But Jimmy isn't a scientist. He's a student of the *yukhyo*, like me."

Danny pulled the car over to the side of the busy road. A few pedestrians shot him a wary look, in case he got the idea to hop the curb and drive down the sidewalk. They quickened their step as they passed the parked car.

An old man dressed in a parking attendant's vest knocked on the window. Danny waved him away. The man took a few steps back and waited, undeterred.

"I thought they were after you because you're some important mathematician," said Danny.

"A faulty premise I'm afraid."

Ye-Rin wore a wide smile. She loved this, seeing Danny being wrong.

"Your father—" said Miles.

"Not my father, Miles. My father is dead," said Danny.

Miles continued unfazed and seemingly unconcerned about the emotional potential of the conversation. "Nevertheless, he seemed very interested in my ability to cope with the probabilities of the *yukhyo*."

"What's *yukhyo*, Miles?" Ye-Rin asked it so sweetly. Danny knew she was just trying to get under his skin. What Korean didn't know *yukhyo*? Even the Christians still believed in the old superstitions.

Miles sounded delighted to be talking about his favorite subject. Danny tuned him out. He rolled down the window and handed the parking attendant a few coins, not enough for the usual half-hour increment. He thought of bribing the old guy, of saying something cool like, "You never saw us." But that kind of thing only guaranteed that the parking attendant would see him and would actively try to find someone to sell his knowledge to. It was better to act pissy and shortchange them.

The man tapped on the door. He motioned with his hand for more. Danny acted as though he were reluctant to pay for a half-hour for what was obviously just a quick stop. Finally, he coughed up the rest of the change.

"So *yukhyo* is like the *I Ching* for Koreans?" Ye-Rin was asking.

"Exactly so, yes," said Miles.

"I get it, and you just roll your little dice? How clever."

"Well, the rolling of the dice is important to the statistical randomness necessary to generate a hexagram, which is a set of lines with an accompanying text. But the real trick is to interpret the writings of the text once you've received the hexagram." He removed a soggy book from his gray jacket pocket.

Danny tried to hijack the conversation. "I thought Christians weren't supposed to go in for witchcraft either."

"Just because we're told not to consult mediums," said Ye-Rin, "doesn't mean they aren't real. Just the opposite. Every witch in the Bible had real powers. Maybe Miles knows what he's talking about. Did you ever think of that Mr. Super-skeptic?"

Danny wasn't a skeptic. To be a skeptic, you had to think there was something worth tearing down. He was a rationalist and a realist. You couldn't be skeptical of the Easter bunny.

"Okay, I'll bite," said Danny. "What was my supposed father so interested in?"

Miles took a moment to respond. "Well, besides your being a spy you mean?"

"Yes."

"He asked me for a reading and was amazed at the result."

"What did he ask you," said Ye-Rin. "A client has to ask a specific question to get a good answer, right?"

So, she did know a thing or two about *yukhyo*, thought Danny.

"Olcha," said Danny, "pull up the image of the man Miles thinks is my father. Put it on the car's navi so we can all see him."

"He asked me if he was going to be successful in a business venture in the near future," said Miles.

The image of an older Korean man was superimposed across the width of the windshield. Ye-Rin put her hand to her mouth. She obviously knew the guy. Every spy in Pyongyang knew him. Now the public did as well.

Miles continued speaking, oblivious to the tension in the car. "The oracle said that he would succeed. It predicted that his victory would not be without sacrifice, as though walking through a fire. He got very excited about my reading."

Olcha played a video on the windshield. It was of the airport bombing and the primary suspect, former North Korean General Park Gee-Man, who was presumed to have blown himself up along with the empty plane. In the video, dancing flames from the burning hull of the jetliner lit the tarmac. Jet fuel was a powerful accelerant, thought Danny, but if it had been rocket fuel, there wouldn't have been enough of the plane left to recognize, much less the nearby terminal full of passengers waiting to board.

It was the same man who had visited Miles's apartment claiming to be Danny's father.

The parking attendant knocked again. This time, Danny ignored him. He was too busy staring in the rear-view mirror at the helmeted face of Miles Birch. What had the man gotten them into?

Chapter 6

So the man who was after you is one of the leaders of the Communist Party in Pyongyang," said Ye-Rin.

"Head of intelligence," said Danny.

"And he was involved in the airport bombing."

"I didn't know that this had anything to do with that, did I Olcha?"

The little program hijacked the car speakers, "Don't look at me, *Oppa*." Her use of the respectful title for an older brother was offset by her sarcastic tone.

Ye-Rin piled on, "Don't try to hide behind your program."

They were moving again, having turned off Revolution Avenue onto one of the side streets that led toward the office complex that housed First Baptist Church of Pyongyang. Some of the streets were narrow, too narrow for two cars to pass at the same time. Yet the drivers of Pyongyang navigated the passages without causing a traffic jam. Danny pulled expertly into a little nook to avoid an approaching dump truck still several blocks down the street. Olcha retracted the car's side mirrors. The compact truck missed them by centimeters. They had to wait while a parade of cars followed the dump truck like a linebacker, using it to clear the way.

Once the convoy was gone, Danny slid back into the road before one of the drivers behind him tried to pass them up. Driving in Pyongyang meant survival of the fittest.

"I didn't know it had anything to do with the bombing, and I sure as hell didn't know that the Party had anything to do with that." Danny added, "Though I will say that if you hadn't gotten cold feet on that case with the biomechanic, what's-his-name—"

"Jeremy," said Ye-Rin, uncrossing and re-crossing her arms. "How you ever survived without me—"

"We were close to a break on the nano-terrorists."

"I couldn't do it anymore."

"I know," said Danny. "You told me."

"But you didn't listen."

"I heard you."

"If you're really heard me, you wouldn't still be playing this game."

"This is not a game. Okay? The leader, well the former leader of Communist Party intelligence knew that I was a spy and came around my place asking some very pointed questions right before blowing himself in a very secure place."

Ye-Rin grew silent. "What are you going to do about it?"

In the past, she would have said what are "we" going to do about it. Danny noticed that there was no "we" anymore, not as far as Ye-Rin was concerned.

He eased past a tight spot where a steel electricity pole stuck up through the pavement. Some joker had decided to park against the wall opposite the poll.

The sedan barely made it through.

Danny finally replied. "To figure out what to do, I need more information. The only question is, who do I ask? The Americans, the Chinese, the Russians?"

"Aren't you an American?" Miles spoke up from the back seat.

Ye-Rin smiled. She always got off on telling this story.

"Even though Danny had American citizenship, he returned to Korea to do his mandatory military service," said Ye-Rin. "He's a patriot."

"So you're Korean-American?" said Miles.

"A *gyopo*," said Ye-Rin. "That's what they call the ones who come back to Korea. Not really a true Korean anymore, not if you abandon the peninsula."

"You're one to talk," said Danny. Ye-Rin had been born in Uzbekistan to parents who were second generation missionaries. Though her parents were still ethnically Korean, Danny felt that, since he'd at least been born on the peninsula before being adopted and taken to America, he had a better claim to Koreanness if she really wanted to play this absurd game.

When they'd dated, their strange origins had been a source of witty banter. Danny didn't like to hear it brought up in front of Miles, who was, after all, a stranger. So, unlike Ye-Rin, he kept his mouth shut about her past.

But he had to say something in his own defense. "I'm not Korean and I'm not American. I'm not really either."

"It's heartbreaking," Ye-Rin was smiling again, laying on the sarcasm nice and thick. Maybe she wanted to get a rise out of him, but there was no reason to respond in anger. Besides, the onscreen navi said they'd be dropping off Ye-Rin after turning onto the next block. There was no point arguing.

Danny stopped the car.

"Why are you stopping, Danny?" said Ye-Rin.

Maybe she was worried he'd try to talk her into staying. Was his presence so repugnant to her now?

"Because I can't get enough of you." Danny rolled his eyes.

He cracked the window, releasing Olcha's drone.

"Olcha, do a flyover of the church," he said.

Superimposed on the windshield's display was the view from Olcha's camera as she rose two stories over the idling car. It felt like an out of body experience, watching yourself as Olcha hovered over you. Then she turned the next corner, orienting on the red neon cross that marked the entrance to the First Baptist Church.

"That's sweet of you, Danny," said Ye-Rin, "But it'd be tough for a spy-hunter to infiltrate a church where everybody knows everybody and where the old *ajuma*s at the front door are nosier than a secretary at Langley."

"But can you reach the front door safely?" said Danny. "Back to your earlier question, Miles, my father told you that I was a spy. Did he not tell you who I worked for?"

"No," said the man. "I just assumed since he said you were raised in America that—"

"That I worked for the Americans," Danny completed his sentence. "A decent assumption."

"Danny works for the Unified Korean government, Miles," said Ye-Rin.

Danny shot her a look.

Ye-Rin shrugged it off. "I'm not a spy anymore. I don't have to keep everybody's secrets."

"Especially since you're reasonably sure I won't kill you?"

"You can't kill me. You owe me a new bike."

Danny shook his head. So that's what this was all about, her getting all prickly and secret spilling.

"I'm sorry about the Vespa," he said.

"Oh, you will be when you see the bill for the expensive replacement."

Olcha had completed a flyover of the front of the church and the surrounding street. Her little drone headed back to the car.

"No. Stay there, Olcha, and walk her to the door."

"It looks safe," said Miles.

He heard a rattling noise coming from the back seat.

"Keep your helmet on, Miles," said Danny automatically. "She doesn't need to see your face when you say goodbye. She won't remember us long enough for it to matter."

Ye-Rin scrunched up her lips as she put on her helmet.

"That's not true," she said. "Olcha, put your feed into my visor." She paused, waiting for the camera to come up on her heads-up display. "I'll remember you, Miles, and the exciting ride we took together. But as for others in the car—"

"Don't go," said Miles.

"That's sweet," she said. "But—"

"You can't walk safely to the door."

Ye-Rin turned to face the strange man. "Why not?"

"The question that Danny asked about whether you can walk to the door safely—I put it to the oracle," Miles pointed to a pair of black dice lying in the floorboard of the car.

So that had been the rattling noise, thought Danny. Miles hadn't been removing his helmet; he'd tossed his dice and rifled though that soggy book.

"You see the hexagram here?" Miles shoved the book into the front seat.

Danny didn't look at the book. His eyes, like Ye-Rin's were focused on the windshield display, looking for a threat.

Danny saw nothing and felt like saying as much. "That *yukhyo* stuff doesn't mean anything."

"Shut up, Danny," said Ye-Rin. "Olcha, switch to infrared and thermal imaging."

Danny grimaced, a little bit chagrined that he hadn't asked for a thermal scan in the first place and grumpy that Olcha hadn't shown more initiative to do it herself. What was the point of a semi-sentient program if she wasn't going to do some of your thinking for you?

The dark street that held First Baptist Church of Pyongyang was suddenly awash in a deep green light. They could see clearly into every nook and cranny in shifting colors of cool greens and yellows as if the street was lit by some alien sun.

A shot rang out.

Olcha shuddered. The view from the camera got shaky.

"Behind the neon cross," said Mal. He spoke through the car speakers. They all looked at the same time. Danny saw a sniper lining up for another shot on the drone that housed his computerized friend.

"Get out of there, Olcha. Evasive maneuvers."

Danny hit the accelerator.

In the parking lot across from the church, headlights came on. Though Olcha was bobbing and weaving through the air, Danny could still see clearly enough, thanks to the image stabilizers. A single figure stepped into the street. He wore new clothing, but the scar over his eye was distinct.

"I should have dropped that *saekki* on the pavement," Danny cursed to himself.

The man waved an arm. A pack of motorcycles turned onto the street, heading in their direction.

The Commies had learned a thing or two since their earlier encounter. For instance, they knew that bikes were better when it came to a chase through the city. They also apparently knew who had helped Miles escape from the YumYum Cafe and exactly how to find her.

"Olcha," said Danny as he negotiated the narrow side streets, "I thought you were keeping tabs on the guy with the scar."

"He must have checked for your bug," said Olcha. "Or maybe he changed shoes considering that you dropped him into the river."

"That's just great. I want to know where he dumped the bug—probably an apartment somewhere—just in case I need to pay him a visit later."

Danny turned to Ye-Rin, who was still wearing her helmet. "I don't think you're going to church tonight," said Danny, as he maneuvered the stolen sedan through an intersection crowded with parked cars. "But you can still pray."

* * *

Danny slammed against a parked car as he took a corner a little too fast. His side view mirrors were lost to the night. He wished Olcha had thought to retract them. But she'd been busy handling her own problems.

"How's it hanging back there, Olcha?" Danny could still see the view from her camera reflected in a corner of the windshield. She was keeping up with the car, and her flight path looked level.

Olcha's on-screen display showed four motorcycles pursuing the black sedan through the side streets of Pyongyang.

"I'm okay number one-*uh*, Danny," said Olcha in her most ridiculous Konglish accent. "He grazed my chassis. Pffft, amateur."

"Ye-Rin would you mind if Mal took over the dashboard, and Miles, lay down across the backseat. I don't want a stray bullet to ruin your night."

"I can handle it, Danny," Olcha pouted. "Up ahead, two more bikes."

"I see them." The two motorcycles were approaching on a perpendicular street a block ahead. They were trying to cut off the sedan. Danny slowed down.

"What are you doing, *Hyung*?" Mal used the term that a younger brother used toward an older brother. "Those motorcycles will box us in."

"Well, you see, Mal," said Danny. "That's the thing about taking on a car with a bike. A motorbike can't stop a car unless the driver really wants to avoid a collision."

Danny hit the gas again, timing it just right so that the black sedan took out the front wheels of the motorcycles as they entered the street. The bikes careened off each other playing pinball with the drivers, knocking them against the side of the car and off the concrete wall of the surrounding building.

"Ye-Rin, how about you make the plan this time. I'm busy."

A muffled voice came out of the backseat. "Why don't we go to the Korean government if you work for them?"

Thankfully, Ye-Rin handled the question. She was no longer taking this in a joking manner. She was probably worried that the thugs had hurt members of her church in their attempt to get at her. It was possible, thought Danny, that they had thugs waiting for her inside. More likely, however, they planned on taking her hostage on the street. Regardless, she'd been thrown in with them. And she might be thinking it was all Danny's fault for involving her in the first place.

Ye-Rin turned toward Miles, to reassure him and also, thought Danny, to get a better view of their pursuers.

"We can't go to the Korean embassy," she said. "They would disavow knowledge of Danny. Plus it would tell whoever is following us exactly who Danny works for. The Koreans might be willing to meet up in private, if we could get a message through; but, even then, they'd probably ignore the message or send a return message expressing confusion and surprise that Danny would be contacting them. It's the usual spy garbage mixed in with the Korean need to save face—especially in a secret operation in the north." Ye-Rin paused. "Danny they're pulling out guns."

Danny had seen the same thing from Olcha's camera angle. He knew from experience how hard it was to drive a bike and shoot a gun at the same time. He'd been doing them a favor by maintaining a straight line. If he didn't want them turning the back of the vehicle, and its occupants, into Swiss cheese, he needed to start making some evasive turns, but where to?

"Turn right," said Ye-Rin, "We go to the Americans."

"Why the Americans? You speak Russian," said Danny, arguing even as he angled onto the next street. "We could go there."

Danny slammed on the brakes. As a bike came racing around the corner, Danny threw the sedan into reverse, sending the trunk of the car into the front tire of the oncoming bike.

The rider hit their back windshield with a sickening crack.

Danny threw the car into drive and peeled out—well, as much as he could peel out in a mid-range civilian sedan. The other three bikes crept around their fallen companion. None stopped to help.

"The Russians are too unpredictable," said Ye-Rin. "They're still sympathetic to the Communists. There's no guarantee they won't turn you in. Same thing with the Chinese, times ten. It has to be the Americans."

"Great," said Danny. "Olcha, give Mal the number for General Sherman Tecumseh Hardis." It was a call he was not looking forward to. Danny had heard that Hardis, his old boss with the U.S. Army, now had deep ties to American intelligence in Pyongyang.

Though Danny was technically a Korean officer, he'd served as a liaison with Hardis's office. The man had tried multiple times to turn Danny into a spy for the American government. He'd given Danny the usual spiel? God, guns, glory and, of course, profit. Plus, he offered the chance to work for what was still the most technologically advanced nation on the planet, though it could no longer claim complete military superiority, having ceded that honor to the BRIC nations (Brazil, Russia, India, China) shortly after the middle of the 21st century, by overextending itself on a number of pointless wars.

In many ways, the march on Pyongyang had been the last hurrah of the famed American military and had succeeded only because, unlike the first attempt one-hundred plus years earlier, they weren't facing millions of screaming Red Chinese.

By the time the Americans had spent manpower and blood taking the capitol, the Russians and the Chinese were already hard at work on factories, racing to become the top suppliers to the nascent rocket industry.

Danny was surprised that the BRIC alliance didn't keep America out of Pyongyang entirely till it was explained to him, in no uncertain terms, that the primary layout in money and market was coming from America. As always, the chief export of the U.S. was capitalism, propelled by pure, unadulterated greed.

Danny spun the steering wheel as the front-most biker put a bullet through the back window.

"Ye-Rin, see if you can stall them while Mal connects us to the General." Danny handed Ye-Rin his pistol. She took it gingerly as though it had just been recovered from a toilet.

"I don't kill people anymore."

"I didn't ask you to kill them," said Danny as he slipped through another tight spot between a pickup truck and a low wall that extended dangerously into the road. He lost some rubber to the bricks on the wall.

"Fine. Open the sunroof, Mal." Ye-Rin checked the gun, making sure it was primed and loaded. "Don't decapitate me, Danny."

"It would only improve your looks."

Ye-Rin leaned out of the top of the car, still wearing her helmet. Danny assumed that Mal was feeding her targets, though she hardly needed any prompting from this range.

The retort of the gun filled the closed interior of the car. Danny's ears rang. A hot shell, expelled from the barrel of the gun, hit him in the side of the neck, sliding down his shirt. The unexpected pain caused him to swerve, putting a huge scratch down the side of a parked BMW.

"Hold still," said Ye-Rin.

"Roll down the windows, Mal," Danny shouted.

The program hesitated.

"Do it," said Ye-Rin.

She withheld fire till the windows began to descend.

Her gun barked. The front tire on the lead bike exploded. The man went over the end of his handlebars and careened off the side of a dumpster.

Ye-Rin refused to kill, but Danny wondered whether a potentially crippling injury was any kinder. Still, at least she was shooting. And she didn't seem to be out of practice.

A gruff voice came over the speakers of the car, "This is General Hardis. Just who in the hell is disturbing me during my dinner hour?"

That was typical of the man, thought Danny, always putting the person across the table on the defensive. Hardis was the sort of man who knew exactly who was calling and, given the amount of time it had taken Mal to get connected to him, Hardis probably had intel up to and including what each of them had for breakfast that morning.

"It's former Lieutenant Danny Kim calling, sir. Sorry to interrupt your victuals." The older man loved it when Danny used colloquial English, the man's eyes would light up in the same way others might when they saw a monkey ride a unicycle.

Ye-Rin opened fire on the remaining two bikes. One of them returned fire, forcing her back into the car.

"Son, it's as loud as a Chinese dumpling shop on fire over there."

Danny had taught him that Korean idiom. "Yes, sir. I seem to have run into a few difficulties and was hoping my old commander might see his way clear to helping us out?"

"What about your old Korean army buddies?"

"Sir, you may recall that I didn't make many buddies." Thanks in part to the man's attempts to ostracize Danny from the other Koreans in his attempts to turn him. The Koreans never trusted Danny's motives in leaving America to perform military service with the Korean Army.

"That's because we are your buddies, Danny. As you are no doubt coming to fully realize."

"Yes, sir."

"Well, in that case, I'd be happy to help out an old friend. Turn onto the next main road."

Danny checked the onscreen navi. They could hit Stalin Street in a few blocks. But turning onto a wide road like that would mean the bikes behind them could pull alongside them and open up on them or on the sedan's unarmored tires.

"Sir—"

"Don't tell me you forgot how to take orders, son."

"No, sir." Danny took the turn. He pushed on the accelerator as hard as it would go and tried to squeeze extra speed out of the steering wheel.

"Ye-Rin, buckle up," said Danny. "Things are about to get interesting."

"Danny," Olcha called out from her spot overhead. "Four more riders approaching on Stalin Street."

"I see them, Olcha," said Danny, sparing a second to look at the world from her perspective. In addition to the four approaching riders, he saw something else that looked interesting. "Olcha, do you see that window repair truck coming up?"

"I do, Danny."

"Mal, take the wheel for a second." Danny ducked into the floorboard scraping past Ye-Rin's exposed knees.

"Hey! Watch it," she said.

Danny pulled a piece of explosive out of his black duffel bag, glad that he'd saved some against emergencies rather than using it all at once on the armored SUV under the bridge. Waste not, want not. He attached a detonator and chucked the entire assembly out of Ye-Rin's window as they passed the repair truck. It stuck to the concrete wall.

"Olcha?"

"Got it."

An explosion decimated the glass panes sitting on the back of the repair truck. Glass went everywhere, breaking the back window of the car, scraping up Danny's neck. He was glad Ye-Rin had been wearing a helmet and that Miles was still lying across the back seat.

Olcha showed him what happened to the motorcycle pursuers. The scene was not pretty. The worst hit had a giant shard of glass sticking out of his stomach. They were no longer a threat. That left only the four bikes coming down Stalin.

The sedan hit Stalin Street at full speed, sending cars swerving to avoid them. Danny turned toward the glowing red arrow that Mal was using to represent the location of General Hardis.

Crossing over the median, Danny barely avoided a weather-stained statue of the dear leader. It stood with its arm raised, wishing them well on their journey.

Behind them, four more bikes roared down the street, joining the chase. Danny didn't know how he was going to avoid the motorcycles on an open road, but the General had asked for a show of good faith and, of course, an act of utter obedience. Well, thought Danny, it was like Hardis always said: beggars couldn't be choosers.

Two of the bikes spread out, ready to overtake the car from both sides, leaving two riders in the rear to box them in.

Ye-Rin reloaded the gun and nodded at Danny. Perhaps she was saying goodbye. The situation looked grim. Maybe she was saying that everything was cool between them now. Sharing a life and death experience could do that.

The first bike moved up, trying to come alongside the passenger's side. Danny swerved to keep the bike behind them, but as he did so, the second bike swung around the driver's side. Cars screeched to a halt at the sight of the rider's raised gun. Ye-Rin chambered a round and emerged from the sunroof, drawing a bead on the rider.

His bike disappeared in a cloud of smoke.

"What was that?" said Ye-Rin.

Mal piped her comment directly into the car's speakers. Danny was wondering the exact same thing. As he looked into the rear-view mirror, two more of the bikes were vaporized, leaving only a flaming crater of asphalt where they'd once been. The fourth bike slammed on its brakes, skidding to a halt. The rider pulled up his visor, showing Danny once again, the scarred face of the man he'd confronted in Miles's apartment.

"That was shock and awe, little lady." General Hardis's voice came over the speakers. Danny hadn't realized that the line was still open. "Shock and awe."

"Talk about killing a mosquito with a canon," said Danny, using another of the General's favorite sayings.

"I told you I got your back, son."

Danny could practically hear the man's smile through the sound system.

"Now, just follow the directions I gave your friend's program. Our drones will provide you with an escort. Be seeing y'all soon."

Those same drones would also prevent Danny from getting second thoughts now that the immediate threat was over. They were on their way to meet with General Hardis, the reputed leader of U.S. intelligence in Pyongyang, but whether that meant they were going to be safe or in even worse danger, Danny couldn't say.

Chapter 7

The fluorescent lights in the underground garage came on as they drove underneath and extinguished as they moved forward, leaving the sedan in a perpetual circle of light. It was a great way to save energy, thought Danny, and worked just as well at freaking out late night visitors.

A voice came over the car's speakers. It was not General Hardis.

"This is MacArthur, General Hardis's assistant program, please park and proceed to the fourth floor. Your companion programs may accompany you but will be quarantined from our system. Leave the drone and all weapons behind, please."

Danny considered the program's name. MacArthur. How like Hardis to have the hubris to name his personal program after the General who had previously beaten North Korea to a standstill. Of course, Hardis had succeeded where MacArthur failed. The Americans had finally taken Pyongyang. Though the country might still

be run by Communists, at least they had come by the
rule honestly, through an American-style democratic
process.

"Miles," said Danny. "You can take your helmet off
now."

"Gladly."

"Olcha," Danny continued giving orders, "I want you
to partition yourself leaving part of you with the drone to
watch the car. Ye-Rin—"

"I can take care of myself," she said, removing her
helmet. Putting her head back, she shook her long black
hair.

She was still so beautiful.

"Get a room, *Oppa*!" Olchaengi teased him as she
might an older brother.

Ye-Rin looked at Danny through narrowed eyes as
she exited the car, sliding her legs out before standing.

"Watch out, *Unnie*, he's going to check out your—"

"Shut up, Olcha," said Danny.

"Fine! But how are you two ever going to get back
together if you won't talk to each other? Somebody has
to say something. Why not me?"

Danny kept the glasses on. He wanted Olcha to have
a way to send messages to him privately, or with as much
privacy as one could hope for in a den of spies. The walls
were full of complex electronic surveillance.

As Danny closed the car door, he noticed for the first
time the extent of the damage the little melee in the
street had caused to the borrowed car. He was going to
owe the owner an explanation—and probably a new ride.
Well, what's one more when he already owed Ye-Rin a
new bike?

Danny replied to Olcha, "You don't get a say about our love life because you are a program."

"Smarter than you," said Olcha. Had she been a physical girl, Danny was sure she'd have stuck her tongue out.

He could see Ye-Rin smiling. Mal was no doubt keeping her up to date on the contents of the conversation.

"Anyways," said Olcha, "I don't need your help, Danny. I have Miles. What about it, Miles? Have you ever given a reading for a program?"

Miles ran a hand through his receding hair. "No, I have not."

"Do you think it would work?" said Olcha.

"I don't see why not."

"My question is this: will Danny and Ye-Rin get back together after this is all over?"

"Don't answer that," said Danny, much as he wanted to know the answer himself, they didn't need a distraction right now.

Ye-Rin led the way. The fluorescents tracked their movement to the far wall, causing them to pass through a tunnel of light. Miles was in the middle. Though Danny carried no weapon, having abandoned his gun in the car, he still insisted on bringing up the rear.

On the wall was a single door for an elevator, one of those old freight elevators where you had to pull the caged door up before entering and pull it down before the elevator would move.

An elevator with its own set of prison bars, thought Danny, this just keeps getting better and better. He hated elevators. And he hated the idea of going to Hardis hat in hand, asking for a favor. Yet here he was.

"Shall we?" said Danny.

As he slammed the door to the ground, Ye-Rin punched the brass button with the number marking the fourth floor. Danny saw her visibly wince. He wondered if there were an electric short, till he saw the control panel. The number four was clearly visible on the button. The Korean number four had the same sound as the word for death. Most Korean elevators avoided the number out of a healthy sense of superstition. Hardis was sending a clear message to the visitors. This way lies death.

The elevator lurched, dragging them upward.

* * *

The smell of cigar smoke permeated the hallway. That was another thing about Pyongyang. Anti-smoking laws had yet to make serious inroads into the country. Aside from Turkey, it was one of the last bastions of conspicuous tobacco consumption. Danny recognized the General's favorite brand of Cuban cigars.

Danny pulled up on the elevator grating allowing their little group to step out onto thin, orangish-red carpet that lined the hallway, barely concealing the concrete underneath. Danny was reminded of the carpeting used around hotel pools. Another message was being sent. They were not being received in style. There would be no oak paneled room waiting for them full of comfortable leather furniture and glasses of scotch.

Instead as they walked down the hallway, the door that stood open offered entry into a chamber that resembled a large interrogation room with gray concrete walls that were entirely bare. The paint on the walls was the same glossy matte that covered U.S. bases worldwide. The high, acrid smell of the government building so easily confused with mold was so indescribably the same.

Inside the dimly lit room were two metal folding chairs arranged in a semicircle. The room was otherwise empty. Danny shook his head at such obvious psychological games. It was meant to make them feel awkward, to wonder which of them should sit in the chairs or if a chair was reserved for the General.

There was no right answer. If two of the chairs were occupied, the General might come in and claim one of them by way of asserting a superior status. Danny could see that Ye-Rin understood perfectly. She studiously ignored the chairs.

They'd been taken to a floor marked death and shown to a room where many guests of the American government might have met a gristly end. The only difference was that they had walked into the room willingly. The only way to handle such a situation was to not play along. You had to act like you owned the place.

Danny folded his hands behind him and adopted a wide stance in the middle of the room with his back to any obvious doors, denying the General the opportunity to make a powerful entrance.

Miles traipsed to the nearest chair and, ignoring it, collapsed in a heap on the floor.

Danny's jaw dropped. Ye-Rin actually laughed a little.

"What? What did I do?" said Miles.

"Nothing," said Ye-Rin. "It's just, things got so intense for a second."

"I've gotten used to floor sitting since I got to Korea. It just feels more comfortable."

Ye-Rin also took a seat on the ground, leaving Danny looking like an alpha male idiot, standing in the middle of the room.

He realized that he didn't know how long he would be standing. If the General saw his pose, which he no doubt would, he'd leave Danny standing long enough to make the preemptive power move uncomfortable.

Danny relaxed and shook his legs out. Miles's, through his obliviousness, had reminded Danny that there was another way to handle these kinds of situations: total and absolute insouciance.

Danny heard the sound of dice rattling. Before he could protest, Miles had his tattered, still-wet book in his hands.

"I'm glad to see y'all making yourselves at home. We did hope you'd be comfortable," The General entered through a concealed door in the wall.

As with any good spy, Danny marked the door in his mind as a possible escape route. Then he realized, with some dismay, that had he still been standing in the middle of the room aping his alpha male fantasies, he would have been facing the door that the General used. He wouldn't have gotten the chance to turn around nonchalantly as the man approached. So, it was just as well that he'd decided to relax with the others.

"Good to see you, General." Danny crossed over to the man with his hand outstretched.

Hardis took it, turning his hand slightly so that the back of his hand faced up. Danny resisted the power play, twisting his wrist to bring both their hands perpendicular to the ground. A subtle game not unlike thumb wrestling developed. Hardis wore a hard smile on his face.

"Yes, good to see you too, Danny. You came here for help, right?"

Danny relaxed his wrist, allowing the General to take the upper hand. It was the first of what Danny knew would be a series of minor concessions that would lead who knew where? He didn't intend to go there without a struggle.

"That's right," Danny said.

Miles was still rolling his dice, seemingly oblivious to the General's entrance. Ye-Rin looked up at the man. She wore an inscrutable expression.

Danny saw that General Hardis had gone to seed. He wore civilian clothes with an olive drab hue that gave off the impression of the military without being an obvious uniform. Hardis's previously taut stomach pushed at the buttons of his shirt. His penchant for whiskey had not been kind to his nose, which had grown rounder and redder since Danny had known him nearly ten years ago. A receding salt and pepper hairline that might have seemed distinguished on another man was worn like a cheap toupee by Hardis.

"Aren't you going to thank me for watching your back when you took out that hit squad at your apartment?"

"You knew about that?" It was a stupid thing to ask. By now the General knew everything related to the night's operation.

"Danny, did you really think those gooks weren't wired to their Red little gills?" said the General.

Danny didn't react to the racial slur. Thankfully, neither did Ye-Rin.

"Hell, son, I've been running interference for you all night. Ever since that yahoo donged on your doorbell." He was gesturing at Miles with the stub of an unlit cigar.

He now took the time to pull a thin butane lighter out of his pocket and relight the burnt end.

"You knew they were coming for Miles?"

"Of course we did, we know everything the Party is doing. Or almost everything." said the General. "Is this the part where we play twenty questions, Danny? If so, I want to take a seat. A real seat." The General sat down in the nearest metal chair with his legs spread wide and one arm over the back. He motioned to the other chair. Danny took a seat in a neutral posture. He wanted information and didn't want to jeopardize the source by playing stupid games of one-upmanship.

"Tell your cute little programs to get ready. I believe we call this an info dump," said General Hardis. "MacArthur," he spoke to his own personal assistant, "pull up the display."

A screen appeared on a wall.

"You recognize this guy?"

A three dimensional portrait floated next to the nearest wall. Behind the picture, an entire dossier of information scrolled by including multiple photos and video coverage of the man inspecting troops prior to the war. They were looking at General Park Gee-Man

"Hey, Danny," said Miles. "It's your dad."

Danny shook his head at the man's complete lack of social grace. Danny didn't know if Miles was trying to make a joke or had genuinely never processed what Danny had repeatedly told him, that General Park was not his father.

Hardis continued, "That's the head of North Korean intelligence. Or it was till earlier today when he suddenly decided to blow himself up."

"We know all this," said Ye-Rin.

"Of course you do," said Hardis. "You Koreans always study so diligently." He paused, waiting for a catty response. Ye-Rin kept her mouth shut. "Do you know why he was at Mr. Miles Birch's fine residence?"

He waited. When Ye-Rin didn't respond, Hardis continued. "That's why Koreans never get ahead. They got smarts, but no imagination."

"He was there for me," said Danny.

"Bingo," Hardis waved a finger in Danny's direction. "See what the fruit of an America education produces? We think he was scoping you out, Danny. Trying to see if he could trust you or turn you. But now we'll never know."

An image of the flaming hull of the destroyed airliner appeared on the wall behind General Park's venerable visage, which slowly faded away, only to be replaced by the man with a scar over his eye.

"You recognize this guy too?"

Danny nodded. Ye-Rin looked confused. Miles didn't seem to care. He was busy rolling his dice and consulting his oracle.

"That's Lee Kang-Sok. He's one evil SOB. He and the General were engaged in a minor struggle for control of the Party's intelligence apparatus." Hardis nodded at the image. "Kang won."

When Hardis referred to a minor struggle, Danny knew exactly what he meant. Minor in the sense that it hardly compared to the politics of maintaining a position in the American agencies. Cutthroat competition for the top jobs was a very literal expression. And Hardis was now at the top in Pyongyang. Danny wondered how many bodies he'd stepped over to get there.

Hardis smiled. "Our people sure got a kick over how you treated that haughty son of a bitch. Your drone came in playing that catchy tune, you busted in on him. Then you were dangling him over the balcony with that look on his face!" Hardis moved his fist back and forth as though he were shaking a rag doll. "And he was all yelling in Korean ching-chang-chong. I almost busted a gut."

Hardis sighed and a great cloud of smoke emerged. "You could've saved me a lot of trouble if you'd dropped him on the pavement."

"You had a chance to vaporize him on the bikes."

"But that would have been tied directly to us; whereas if you'd done it—"

It occurred to Danny that Hardis might have engineered the whole thing. "You knew Kang was after Birch and that I was right next door."

Hardis smiled. "Not I," said Hardis. "General Park was after you. He met Miles. Then Kang-Sok wanted to know why the old General had consulted a fortuneteller. You know how superstitious the Koreans are?" Hardis motioned to Danny with the hand that held the burning cigar. "Walk with me for a second."

Ye-Rin started to rise too.

"No need Miss Moon. This is a man-to-man talk."

Though Ye-Rin carried no weapons, Danny was mildly surprised that she didn't attack Hardis with her bare hands for an insult like that. Maybe her Christian faith was having a real effect on her.

Danny and the General stepped out into the thinly-carpeted hallway. Like all American government buildings, the walls were marked with lines of various colored paints, so that even in the face of some very difficult conditions, the occupants could find their way around. There were some things that technology could not replace including certain fail-safes like these.

A thick hand still calloused from use rested on Danny's shoulder. "We worked together a long time, son. I trust you. Even though you're on the other side."

Danny started to object, but Hardis warded him off with the wave of a hand. "I know you don't see it as the other side, but there's us and there's not us. That's the way it's always been."

They took a few steps in silence. "I know why you did it. You wanted to show your loyalty to the country where you were born. But they never did accept you, did they? That's how they are, son. You and your girl from Uzbekistan. So true to the gooks and receiving no thanks."

Danny couldn't object, not even to the pejorative term. Native Koreans called Danny a *gyopo*, which was worse than any insult the General could use.

What the man was saying was true. Danny had joined the Republic of Korea Army even though, as a U.S. Citizen raised abroad, he had no obligation to undergo mandatory military service. However, even though he had volunteered, and despite his efforts to fit in, they never treated him like he was one of them, even though he was the same race and his blood was as Korean as any of them. Ye-Rin had experienced something similar. Their shared sense of isolation had drawn them together.

"I know what it feels like," continued General Hardis. They reached the end of the long hallway and turned a corner. "I moved to the Appalachian Mountains when I was a teenager. I know that I sound Southern, but daddy was a Yankee. We moved back to my mom's hometown of Grundy, Virginia where my dad took a job teaching at a local college. Even though all my family was from there and most of them still living there, you think those kids ever treated me like I belonged?"

"It's not as though I fit in in America either, sir," said Danny.

Hardis cut him off. "You did fine in America. Or you could have, if you didn't have that chip on your shoulder. Everyone can find a place in America because it's an idea, son, not a race. It's like the man said, the difference between Americans and Koreans is that anyone can become an American."

Hardis squeezed Danny's shoulder affably. It was the same old sales pitch. Danny stared straight ahead. There was nothing new to say.

"Danny, I need your help." Hardis removed his hands and showed both palms to Danny, in a way that said wait, let me explain.

"General Park and Kang-Sok didn't see eye to eye. They were fighting over the use of some new weapon in their terror tactics—you know, to restore North Korea to its natural heritage and all that crap."

The idea didn't sound entirely unreasonable to Danny, who'd been reminded on almost a daily basis in the Korean army about the evils of occupation under the Japanese in the previous century. Koreans were ones to hold a grudge.

"The Party developed a new bomb, completely undetectable. The General was loathe to use it, not wanting to slaughter innocent Commie bystanders." Hardis smiled at his joke. He thought he'd made an oxymoron. "Kang is one of those ideological, any means necessary, kind of bastards. You know the type, charismatic, but not willing to play nice with the rest of us? Not minding collateral damage."

Danny nodded in acknowledgement.

"We think Kang-Sok found a way to get rid of his opposition and test the new bomb at the same time."

They turned another corner. Hardis motioned Danny into another room. This one was well lit and lined with computer screens. Danny could see that the cameras were focused on the two prisoners sitting in a near-empty holding cell: Ye-Rin and Miles.

Again, Hardis was hardly being subtle. Danny recognized the implicit threat in the present arrangement. Hardis was about to hit Danny with a serious request. If Danny balked, the lives of Ye-Rin and of Miles were at stake. Though in some ways, it seemed a weak move. Hardis had to know how little he cared about his next door neighbor. And Ye-Rin had broken up with him. Hardis must be grasping if he was willing to make a play based on such poor leverage.

Hardis pointed at a wall with his cigar. It had gone out again due to lack of attention. The picture of the burning aircraft appeared at his command.

"Danny, we're not exactly sure how this happened. And you know how much we know."

The Americans, while undergoing a bit of a hiccup in terms of military dominance, yet retained a significant technological lead. The Unified Korean government, virtual tributary that it was to D.C., relied heavily on the forensic work of their American partners.

Butane flowed from the tip of Hardis's thin lighter as he re-warmed the end of his cigar, pulling on it with a few deep drags till it came to life again.

"Their bugs took out the fuel truck. It was full of high test petroleum. The General had been smuggled on board, alive, before any other passengers were allowed to board the plane. We monitor the airport constantly as you probably know. " Hardis exhaled smoke. "We recovered some of the nano-bugs that did the job. But they're unlike anything we've ever seen before. We can't get a bead on them. They keep mutating."

"Where do I come in, sir?"

"Well," Hardis smiled, "since your cover is blown anyway, we asked for a friendly loan of your services from the Korean government. They were only too happy to oblige."

Since they have to do what you Americans say, thought Danny, of course they complied. Most of his agency probably thought he was a double agent for the Americans anyway. Hardis's request would confirm their suspicions.

"I see you're thinking like me that they'll probably never take you back after all this," said Hardis, "but I'm here to tell you that your Uncle Sam would never treat a valuable asset like this. If we don't like you, we have the class to put a bullet in your head ourselves."

Danny thought about playing hardball, about saying something petulant. But it was all a foregone conclusion. His government had sold him over to Hardis in return for who knew what promises. Hardis was finally going to get what he always wanted, for Danny to belong completely to him.

"You want me to go after Kang-Sok? Get the weapon or destroy it. Is that about it?"

"See, that's what I always loved about you. So direct, unlike all the rest of these gook bastards. No offense."

"None taken, sir. What kind of support can I expect?"

"Support?" Hardis looked almost offended. "As if a top gun like you needs help from us?"

Hardis took on a thoughtful look, "We can't do anything direct, mind you, but we can keep up the sort of low level interference we've been running. For instance, we can't keep you off of facial recognition, but we can overwhelm the system with false positives. Beyond petty shit like that, you're on your own. You're a resourceful young man. This can't have our fingerprints on it."

"You mean besides those gaping holes in the pavement where those bikes used to be."

"But you'll also note that we didn't touch Kang-Sok. He knows that we can't touch him without causing a major incident. But you can. You and your little buddies."

Danny looked at the computer screen that held the images of Ye-Rin and Miles.

"No deal," said Danny. "Ye-Rin has taken a vow not to kill. And Miles is an American citizen. He's your problem now."

"Tsk, tsk, tsk," Hardis clucked his tongue at Danny. "Leave him here if you like, I don't care," said Hardis, "but don't blame me if I trade his crazy ass to the Party in return for some top agents they're holding."

"You wouldn't. He has valuable information that they want. He's a theoretical mathematician."

"He's worth nothing to us, don't you see? He's like a tarot card reader working out of a shopping mall in the poor part of town," said Hardis. "But, since General Park's visit, the Party thinks he's the damn second coming of the Messiah or something. You keep him alive if that's what you want, or trade him for info on Kang-Sok. I don't really care if he lives or dies."

"But he's an American," said Danny.

"Son, America is bigger than any one person. Especially a person who chose of his own free will to abandon our fair shores for some run-down piss-hole apartment in Commieville."

Danny didn't bother pointing out that he lived in the same apartment complex.

"And Ye-Rin?"

"She's free to go," said Hardis. "Of course, it won't be a minute till the Party picks her up. What do you think they'll do with a former honeypot like her? Doesn't take a lot of imagination, does it?"

Danny tried not to get his back up.

"Look," said Hardis, "you do your job right, and we'll take care of your girl and even Mr. Miles Birch." He clapped Danny hard on the shoulders.

The unspoken implication was that the converse was also true. If Danny failed, Hardis would feed Ye-Rin and Miles to the Party without blinking. What were they to him? A geek and a whore. No more, no less.

"You and Ye-Rin, this is your old beat. I'm reliably told that you had a line on some of these new terror weapons before your team got shut down."

Danny couldn't deny it. They'd been close to turning one of the top illegal biomechanics in the city, getting a line on who'd been cranking out the nano-bombs, till Ye-Rin got cold feet.

"Kang-Sok is out there, Danny. He's plenty pissed at you. You're only doing yourself a favor by taking the bastard out. And it just so happens that you'd be doing me a favor as well, and I like to reward those who do favors for me."

The video image on the wall played a drone flyover of the burning wreck of the airliner. Danny watched the plane from all angles. If Kang-Sok was as dangerous as Hardis said, not that he could trust the man to give him the full truth, but if Kang-Sok had a new kind of explosive, then he was sure that his handlers with the Unified Korean government would be just as interested as the American government. Their interests seemed to coincide.

"I'll do it."

"Good. We've got intel that Kang-Sok is planning something big in the next week. So don't dilly-dally." Hardis smiled. He held out a hand. "Welcome to the team, son."

Even as Danny took the man's hand, allowing his to be turned over slightly so that Hardis's hand could dominate, he thought to himself: I am not your son. And if you are lying to me, General Hardis, Kang-Sok won't be the only one I take out. He smiled cordially at Hardis who took the smile as a confirmation of their fast friendship.

The General led him through the side door to his friends. Ye-Rin would know what that meant, thought Danny, that I'm on the inside now.

Who could tell what Miles made of the situation? He was throwing dice like he was running a craps game in an alley. The man had no idea how much danger his habit had gotten him into. The mild-mannered mathematician was now in on the hunt for one of the most dangerous men in Pyongyang.

Chapter 8

The streetlights of Pyongyang bounced off the windows of the black Hyundai sedan as it rolled down the large thoroughfare leading to Reunification Square—wind whipped through the back window, which had been blown out earlier in the evening.

Danny was at the steering wheel again. Red and orange neon lights reflected off his face, shining on the clear glasses that connected him to Olchaengi, his companion program. He could remember a time when neon lights had been as rare as democracy in the north. Now, the closer the car came to the square, the more the streets resembled Seoul's Gwanghwamun Square or Japan's Hachiko Square—just another hub of Asian commerce and culture. Large screens blared out advertisements: rocket trips to the moon or a suborbital cruise above the north pole among the aurora borealis, mixing with ads for designer fashion and handbags.

Those wealthy enough to enjoy the shopping at Revolution Square strolled on sidewalks thick with pedestrians and with city police. It seemed as likely a place as any to get lost in a crowd.

Danny turned into the underground parking garage of the Tan-Gun Hotel, one of the first five star establishments to open in a city that had just begun to cater to the newly wealthy space entrepreneurs. It also happened to be the place Olchaengi had identified as the hideout of Kang, based on the tracker Danny had put on him before dropping him into the Taedong River.

The guard at the bottom of the ramp gave the beat-up sedan a disapproving look as though its shabby state might reflect poorly on the high-end European cars lining the top floor of the garage. Danny had half a mind to hand the car over to valet parking just to piss the man off. But that would create another eyewitness once the car was eventually discovered. It would take some time before that happened. Even now, Olchaengi was hacking the parking lot security system, hiding any evidence of their arrival, deleting their pictures and the car from the database. Maybe if they got out of this alive, he would have Olcha drop the car owner a line letting her know where she could find the car. Or maybe he would have General Hardis make an anonymous donation to the woman's bank account.

Ye-Rin had been silent during the drive to the hotel. Danny didn't know how to interpret her mood. She didn't want to be involved in all this, he knew. But she had no choice now. They had to see it through together.

Miles, of course, had kept himself busy consulting the oracle. Danny didn't ask what about. He didn't want to know. The only reason the man was still along for the ride was that Danny had enough experience with Hardis to know the General had not been bluffing about trading

Miles to the Party. Neither did he think Miles would survive more than a day on his own in the city. Even with the Americans providing subtle counterintelligence, Miles was bound to do something stupid like he'd done in the YumYum Cafe, paying for his drink with a personal card or going back to the office for a file he'd forgotten.

"Danny, I pulled the information you wanted off the parking lot security system." Olcha was talking through the car's speakers, addressing them all. She flashed a series of images onto the windshield. They showed Kang riding into the underground garage astride a black motorbike. The timestamp on the image indicated that Kang had preceded them into the Tan-Gun Hotel by less than three hours.

"There's a good chance he's still here," said Danny. Once given an assignment, his OCD nature took over, making him itch to see the thing through to its conclusion. It was one of the things that made him both a good agent and a terrible boyfriend.

"Good, let's get this over with," said Ye-Rin.

This mission must be infringing on her new life of quiet meditation.

Danny parked the car on the lowest level, seven floors under the hotel. He rolled down the window and released Olcha into the closeted air of the parking garage.

"Keep an eye out for any unwelcome visitors," Danny told the drone. "Ye-Rin, you think Mal is up to hacking the hotel's security system? I'm concerned he might be rusty."

"I can handle a *geojigatun* security system," said Mal defensively.

Danny held up his hands in mock surrender. "Go to it then."

"*Nuna*?" Mal was still asking for permission. It annoyed Danny a little that Ye-Rin hadn't authorized Danny to give simple commands to her program.

"Go ahead, Mal." Ye-Rin leaned back in the passenger's seat, closing her eyes.

So this was the team he was supposed to work with to take down the Party's main operator? Either General Hardis thought highly of Danny or was setting him up to fail. It wouldn't surprise Danny to learn that he was just one of many irons that Hardis had in the fire on a mission of this much importance.

"Ok, *Hyung*, check this out." Mal demonstrated his prowess. Within seconds, the hotel guest list was scrolling across the windshield display while hotel cameras were being accessed in a secondary display. Mal was running a complex facial recognition algorithm.

"I've got him," Mal gloated. "He's in the adjoining casino."

A live image of Kang appeared, taking over the main display. He was seated at a Go-Stop gaming table in the casino looking rather dour and nursing a highball. Although Danny had seen the man before, he'd never actually taken the time to study him.

There was much more to his face than the scar that ran over the top of his eyebrow. He had high cheekbones that lent a lean, hungry look to a profile that was otherwise delicate. Kang had a definite air of femininity to his face. In his prepubescent days he might have been mistaken for one of the effeminate K-Pop stars that Olcha so treasured.

"Okay, let's take him," said Danny.

"I don't think that's a good idea," said Miles.

Danny's eyebrow shot up as he looked at the man through the rearview mirror. "And why is that, Miles?"

"The oracle says that we should wait."

"Could the oracle be more specific?"

"Yes, actually. I inquired as to the probabilities regarding our current mission and the oracle assured me that, mathematically, our best chance would be for Ye-Rin to capture Kang at 11:07 p.m. in an access corridor leading to the casino's kitchen."

"Why not Colonel Mustard with the candlestick in the library?"

"Excuse me?" said Miles.

"Danny's being sarcastic, Miles," said Ye-Rin, opening her eyes.

"I understood the reference to the classic board game Clue," said Miles, "I just didn't—"

"How could the oracle be so specific?" said Danny.

"I asked it some very specific questions and triangulated the answers, testing them systematically. What do you think I have been doing this entire time?"

"Let it go, Danny," said Ye-Rin. "There's another reason we can't move in on Kang right now."

"Is the oracle speaking to you too now? Or did the holy spirit whisper in your ear?"

"Mock my beliefs all you want," said Ye-Rin. "You can't argue with facts."

She hadn't reacted at all to his jibe. When they'd been dating, that remark would have drawn an angry protest. But then, she'd been conflicted, torn between her job and her faith.

She pointed at the screen. "Kang has got some serious backup. That, in addition to the hotel security means our little team has no chance at taking him. Maybe if we had an extraction team and a month to plan—"

"But we don't," said Danny. "Hardis says that Kang has a weapon and that he's going to use it, sooner rather than later."

Ye-Rin finally sat up and looked at Danny. There was no love to temper the scorn in her eyes. "The airport bombing?"

"Yes," said Danny. "Hardis said it was something new. Something they'd never seen before."

"You trust Hardis?"

Danny had mulled that thought over during the silent drive to the hotel.

"I don't *not* trust him. He's obviously setting us up. He's always working wheels within wheels." Danny paused. "But, look, my cover in Pyongyang is blown. I'm done here thanks to that *jasig* in the backseat. This could be my last mission in the field. I want to see it through."

"You could quit."

"Like you?" said Danny. "It would take an act of god."

"Stranger things have happened," said Ye-Rin.

Danny was rapidly tiring of this conversation. "Look, just because we can't take Kang doesn't mean we can't talk to him."

"Danny, you can't be serious."

"Why not? Like you said, the casino security is tight. They won't let anything happen inside."

"What about when you try to leave? Kang will be waiting to slit your throat as soon as your feet hit the pavement."

"Not if you and Miles get to him at 11:07 like the oracle says, or don't you believe it?"

"Fine," said Ye-Rin. "Get yourself killed." She made an obvious display of checking the time before slumping back against the seat, feigning sleep.

I love you too, thought Danny, as he opened the car door. He left his black leather jacket in the car, along with his gun and his favorite Doosan Bears baseball cap. Thankfully he hadn't changed out of his work clothes, a stylish pair of black trousers and a slick, purple v-neck long sleeved shirt. One thing about running security for an expensive company like Next Wave, Danny should fit right in with the high-rolling casino crowd.

"Miles, keep her out of trouble okay?" he said. "Olcha, you and your drone walk with me. We're going to win a little money."

Chapter 9

The security setup at the casino was standard fare. Thuggish, genetically modified guards stood at the doors lending the personal touch to any quests who might think about causing trouble. But the real muscle lay in the technology hidden in the walls and ceiling. The casino had superb surveillance attached to the latest emotio-ware that tracked the visual and biorhythmic output of the guests.

The operators knew who to feed coffee to in order to keep them plugging away at the slot machines and who to ply with alcohol to boost a sense of invincibility at the roulette tables. They also knew, within probabilities, who was lying and who was cheating. The security could stop a fight before the aggressor threw the first punch.

"No drones, sir," said one of the meatheads.

"It's my seeing-eye drone," said Danny. "I'm legally blind without her." He held out his wallet toward the guard which indicated that Danny was blind as a bat and required assistance from the drone at all times. The guard looked at the card. Danny was sure that the card was being scanned and its contents verified.

Danny had also caused his eyeglasses to go completely dark before entering the casino, which was a nice touch, if he did say so himself.

He knew the security system was probing him. He was lying, but as a spy, he'd been trained to lie with every breath.

"Keep it out of the air, sir."

"You heard the man, Olcha."

The drone settled onto Danny's shoulder like a pet parrot. He looked around the casino through his own eyes and also through the camera feed that Mal was sending his way.

Casinos were a ubiquitous attachment to most fancy Asian hotels and reflected the opulence of the establishment. Gold gilding and bright lights were de rigueur. Danny avoided the slot machines and the roulette tables. Neither blackjack nor poker held any interest for him. These were meant to fleece the tourists. Instead, Danny walked casually toward the back of the casino where the traditional Korean games were being played.

He stepped past the party goons that were flanking Kang's table. They didn't move to stop him. They were entirely too trusting of the casino security, thought Danny. They knew he didn't have a weapon. You had to bribe the casino to get a weapon past security. Danny saw the outlines of some major hardware on the goons' hips, under their jackets. He also assumed they had bribed the casino enough to alert them should anyone else be carrying a weapon.

Danny wondered briefly if General Hardis was, like Mal, watching the proceedings from a safe location and, if so, what the man thought was about to go down.

The other player stood up, cursing in a heavy northern dialect. He slammed his cards on the table. Kang regarded the man with a slightly amused expression. Winning some money must have changed Kang's bad attitude. In games of Go-Stop, large amounts of cash could change hands quickly.

The loser stormed past Danny, who slipped into the unoccupied seat.

Kang collected his winnings. He hadn't looked up at the newcomer. Here was the man who was supposed to be the head of intelligence for the Communist Party, staying in the nicest hotel, winning large stakes at the gaming tables. Danny knew about the hypocrisy of the Party leaders, but could never quite get over it.

"I see you've dried off considerably since we last met."

Kang's eyes widened. His lip curled. He reached into his jacket for a weapon.

Immediately, Kang's chest lit up with laser targeting dots. Huge guns with rotating barrels snaked out of concealed compartments in the casino's gilded ceilings. The dealer ducked under a table that had no doubt been reinforced. Kang's guards moved forward.

"I wouldn't do that if I were you, Comrade," said Danny, nodding toward the man's chest. "I haven't threatened you. The casino might look askance at your shooting me at their table. Not good for their reputation."

Danny doubted whether Kang's bribes to the casino covered murder.

"You're a dead man." Kang's hand relaxed on his weapon. He waved away his guards.

"So you told me last time. Yet here I am."

"If the Americans hadn't interfered, I would have had you and your *gyopo* whore."

"The Americans owed me a favor," said Danny, remaining calm. He waved two fingers at the dealer, who had just peeked out from under the table, signaling that she should deal him in. "I'll start with ten thousand dollars." Olcha began handling the financial transaction.

"We don't play for American money here. Only Korean Won."

"How patriotic of you," said Danny. "Ten thousand Won, then." He did the calculation in his head. The dollar was sitting at about half the value of the Won now.

Kang smiled and, as he did so, the scar on his eye shifted, giving him a more mischievous look. "Are you sure that will be enough? We play for a thousand Won per point at this table."

"I'm sure I can handle it." To the dealer he added, "Any house rules I should know about?"

The dealer shuffled the thick cards expertly, not in a cascade of cards like they might at a blackjack table, but in a quick movement of short stacks from top to bottom. At a traditional, family game, one of the players would have dealt, chosen by luck of the draw. In a game of chance, outside the trusted walls of the family estate, however, a dealer was something of a necessity to prevent the more obvious forms of cheating.

The dealer spoke as she shuffled, "*O gwang*, or collecting the five bright cards counts as fifty points at these tables, sir; otherwise, the rules follow the standard casino variation."

Kang interrupted, "If that's too rich, you can play baccarat."

The dealer concluded, "Are you familiar with the casino variant?"

"I am." Danny signaled that the dealer should deal the hand. He addressed Kang as the first four cards of the draw pile hit the table face up. "In return for their favor, the Americans asked me to do them a favor as well. I have to get my hands on the bomb you're planning on using."

The dealer nearly dropped the cards she'd pulled off the top of the deck for Danny. Adroitly, she recovered, handing the five cards to Danny and five more to Kang before adding another four, face up, to the draw pile.

She dealt both Danny and Kang five more cards and stacked the deck neatly directly between the two players. To Danny, being handed all his cards at once was unsettling, considering the western tradition he'd grown up with where the cards were dealt to each player alternately.

The view from the casino's cameras, courtesy of Mal, showed the two men sitting at the gaming table, a stack of unused cards between them. Eight cards lay face up on the table, forming a draw pile from which they could make matches.

The setup reminded Danny of the games of Go Fish he'd played back in America. But in the Korean game of Go-Stop, cards could be combined in infinite arrangements, with each type of combination worth a certain amounts of points. Add to that the ability to steal cards from the other player's collection or the way certain combinations doubled or tripled one's score, and fortunes could change rapidly.

Danny examined his hand, holding it tightly to his chest so that Kang couldn't spy on him if he happened to have hacked into the casino's camera in the same way Mal had done.

Kang did likewise. Danny couldn't get a peek at Kang's cards through the cameras Mal was feeding into his glasses. Neither would any of Olcha's optical tricks work on the casino's cards. The thick cards, almost tile-like in their weight, were insulated against any such snooping.

His cards weren't bad. He had some promising animal combinations as well as ribbons. He spied some matches between the cards in his hand to those in the draw pile. Olcha began scrolling probabilities in the corner of his glasses. She figured he had a slight advantage.

Danny played first. He picked a match to his plum set from the draw pile and moved it and the card in his hand to the table in front of him. He finished his turn by drawing a card from the remaining stack. It too was a plum.

"Unlucky," said Kang as Danny was forced by the rules to move his collected plum set along with the drawn card back into the draw pile. Whoever drew the final plum card would get a complete set.

Play continued as Kang collected a set from the draw pile before picking a new card from the deck. Unable to use it to form a combination, he discarded it.

"What makes you think I'm just going to give you the weapon?" Kang smiled at the absurdity of the idea.

"I can give you Miles Birch." Danny played calmly as though they were sitting in the kitchen back home.

"That's not very neighborly of you." Kang collected an animal card. He had two birds in front of him. One more would give him a *godori*, a rare and valuable collection.

"We were never very close neighbors," said Danny. "If he hadn't barged in on me this evening, I never would have gotten involved in this *asulajang*, this boondoggle."

"I could not exchange the weapon for that fake *chomjaengi*," said Kang.

"If he's a fake, how did he tell me where to find you?" Danny lied. "And why were you so interested in him in the first place?"

"That's hardly your concern."

"You said I'm a dead man, so why not tell me?"

"Your interrogation will not work, Do-Song. I am not a stupid American villain on the movies."

"No," said Danny, "you're not even that bright."

Danny drew from the deck, collecting the top card along with the card Kang had just discarded, forming a full set of ribbons. He had a choice to make. He had seven points, enough to call a "stop" to the game. But if he said "go," the game would proceed, allowing him to build on his already large sets, earning more points and possibly doubling, tripling or quadrupling as many times as he kept saying "Go." But if Kang got even the minimum points necessary to call "Stop," Danny's greed would be assessed against him.

Danny counted in his head. His points along with the penalty that would be assessed against Kang for leaving cards on the table equaled a tidy sum.

The choice was simple. If he won too big, too early, Kang might abandon the table. He needed to give the man an incentive to stay so that he could milk him for information or deliver a more crushing blow.

"Stop," said Danny. He would lure Kang in, get him on the next game.

"20,000 Won to Kim Do-Song *neem*," said the dealer, using the honorific.

Kang's fist hit the table.

Olcha registered the receipt of the money minus the ten percent fee the casino took out of all private winnings.

"Tell you what," said Danny, as he collected the chips from the table. The transfer of money had already been made electronically, the chips served as a cool prop, to make the winner feel big. "We're a couple of gambling men. Why don't we play for it? First one to, say, 250,000 Won wins? If I win, you give me the weapon. If you win, Miles and I come with you."

Danny didn't need the casino's emotio-ware to see that he'd struck a nerve. The intense stare from Kang looked as though the man had been waiting his whole life to gamble for such high stakes. What spy hadn't fantasized about taking a seat at the table across from James Bond in Casino Royale? Or maybe Kang was like one of those fabled big game hunters that wanted to track the ultimate prey: man.

* * *

"We should be going now."

Ye-Rin opened her eyes. The mathematician was still in the back seat. He would have done everyone a service by having the decency to walk away from the mess he'd created. The Party could capture him and life could go back to normal. For that matter, Ye-Rin questioned why she was still sitting in the car. The Party had ID'd her from her dramatic rescue of Miles. But she could still go to ground, hide out for a while. She could go to one of the prayer mountains; she might find peace in one of those remote retreats. She might never come back.

"It's a quarter till eleven. We have twenty-two minutes or thirteen hundred and twenty seconds, minus one, minus one, minus one—"

"Spit it out, Miles."

"We should be moving into position. That's how you spies say it, right?"

"I'm not a spy anymore, Miles."

"Right, right, found the one way, the three in one, a theoretical theological puzzle."

"Miles, if we stay in the car, are you going to keep talking?"

"Probably. I've asked the oracle everything I can. I need fresh data."

That did it. Ye-Rin couldn't sit in the car with Miles. Danny was about to get tactical support whether he wanted it or not. Ye-Rin held the gun in her lap. The metal barrel weighed heavy on her legs, heavy on her soul. She briefly considered handing it to Miles, but that seemed a more dangerous prospect than going out unarmed. Ye-Rin placed the gun under her seat. She'd told Danny that she'd never kill again.

Out of the saddle bags she'd salvaged off the Vespa before drowning it in the Taedong River, Ye-Rin pulled out a pair of designer eyeglasses.

She rifled through Danny's duffel bag looking for anything useful. He had a radar deflector and a few small pieces of the explosive he'd thrown past her face out of the car window.

That had been a much closer call than she cared to think about. The explosive had flown not three centimeters past her nose.

She took a small piece of explosive and a combination trigger with inbuilt tremolo switch, photoelectric switch, or the trigger could be activated remotely.

"Mal, part of you stay here with the car; keep an eye on our gambler and on the security system. The rest of you come with me."

Ye-Rin took one last look at the display in the car windshield. It showed Danny sitting down with Kang. He'd never lacked for courage, that was sure. She remembered the first time he'd approached her at the pistol course at the shooting range outside of Seoul. He'd been so cute, so cocky; so totally unlike anything her parents had been. They were stoic people, third generation missionaries eking out an existence in Uzbekistan. Ye-Rin had been sent to the States for high school and then shipped off to Seoul to live with an aunt and to study medicine. The first thing she learned is that she didn't mind cadavers. The second thing she learned was that medical school was expensive. She'd gotten way in over her head in debt. Then she'd been recruited. The agency had used her debt against her, used it to make her do things she didn't care to think about anymore.

Her thoughts drifted as she exited the car and waited for Miles to join her. His gray jacket held as many wrinkles as the Rangnim Mountains. His thinning brown hair and sallow complexion spoke to a lack of exercise.

She asked him, "Your oracle says that we have to go to the access corridor to the kitchen?"

"Did you want to cross-correlate my data with your Holy Spirit?"

"Are you joking?" said Ye-Rin. Yet the man had said it without a hint of a smile.

"Studies show that people of faith are more intuitive than those who lack faith. I was merely trying to utilize your parlance to ask whether you had any sense of agreement."

"Let me ask God real quick," Ye-Rin shut her eyes. "Nope, nothing." She opened them again, glaring at Miles.

"I only meant—" Miles trailed off.

She could see that he'd genuinely meant it when he'd asked about the Holy Spirit. And she, good Christian that she was, had thrown it right back in his face. The fact was, she hadn't been praying as much as she ought to that night. Maybe it was being back with Danny. Or maybe she was falling into old patterns of self-reliance.

She'd also missed a chance to share her faith with another human being. She felt vaguely guilty for not proselytizing him. The pastors said you had to boldly proclaim the Gospel no matter where you were. Ye-Rin would rather have her life serve as an example. Anyone could say what they believed, but few could actually live it. She had determined to act consistently with her re-found faith. As sure as she'd acted as an agent for the Unified Korean government; she was now an agent for Christ.

The lines around Ye-Rin's eyes softened. "I'm sorry, Miles. It's just that God doesn't talk to me like that. I keep asking, but I'm not hearing anything back."

"The oracle says—"

Ye-Rin held her hands up in a non-controversial stance. "I don't need a direct line of communication. I have the Bible. If I can read it and follow it, that's enough."

"Bible numerology is a fascinating field of study," said Miles.

Bless him, thought Ye-Rin; he was trying to find some common ground to talk about.

He continued, "Did you know that if you assign numbers to the various names of God in the Hebrew alphabet, and then multiply them times—"

Ye-Rin interrupted. "Tell me about it on the way. We've got to go right?"

"Fifteen minutes and thirty seconds or—"

"I get it. Let's walk." Ye-Rin steered him toward a stairwell.

* * *

"So you see," said Miles, "the number six-sixty-six derives from the number of fallen man, which is six, multiplied by the number of Satan, also six, to form 36, then if you add 36 to 35 to 34 and so forth down to one, you receive the number of the Anti-Christ, six sixty-six."

Getting out of the car had not shut Miles Birch up. The man had talked incessantly up the stairwell and down the halls that separated the front of the house from the back of the house at the casino.

Ye-Rin had expected some kind of challenge to their entrance into the serving corridors. Yet no guard had been posted, no electronic warning had flown into her field of vision. More importantly, no guns had dropped out of the ceiling.

Neither had they been accosted by waiters moving in and out of the kitchen. At this late hour, the tip money was in drinks.

Ye-Rin located the kitchen and the hallway that ran around the perimeter of the casino, containing swivel doors that let out in many places onto the casino floor.

She wondered exactly which door they should be waiting at. She decided that it should be the one closest to Danny and to Kang.

Absent the security shake down she'd been expecting, Ye-Rin was free to ignore sneaking and subtlety, free to ignore Miles, and to focus on the feed from the casino's cameras. Danny was playing the most intense game of Go-Stop she'd ever seen. It wasn't a sedate game like poker where the two opponents tested each other, developing the game slowly to a dramatic finish.

Instead, the two players were flying through the small multi-colored cards. Her mother had tried to teach her how to play. The lessons had not stuck. The scoring system was far too complicated. It would take a woman playing twenty Bingo cards at once to replicate the level of concentration involved in tracking the possible combinations. Not that there wasn't room for bluffing. Especially in the endgame.

Ye-Rin saw Danny's collection on the table. She read his hand through the feed Olcha provided form where she sat on his shoulder.

She heard Danny say one word. "Go."

Ye-Rin couldn't believe it. He could have stopped and was taking a risk, trying to earn more points.

Of course he was, she thought. He'd promised to go to his death if he didn't win the game. He was playing like his life was on the line for the simple reason that it was. Danny had proposed to trade himself and Miles should he lose. Actually, maybe Miles should be wearing the glasses, thought Ye-Rin. He would no doubt have a much better grasp of the math involved.

"Miles?" She interrupted his lesson on the numerological origins of the number 777. "Do you know how to play the game Go-Stop? The one Danny's playing?"

Miles chewed at his lower lip. "Fascinating in its probabilities. But sadly I devoted my time to learning the subtle science of the *yukhyo*, though the flower cards of Go-Stop, also called *godori*, do have interesting connections to Tarot cards in that—"

"Miles. Hush." Ye-Rin covered his mouth with her hand.

As they rounded a corner toward the exit nearest Danny, passing trays piled high with dirty dishes from where tables had been bussed but never delivered to the dishwashers, Ye-Rin saw a man in a dark suit standing against the wall next to the swinging door that let servers into the casino.

She lost track of Danny's game as she concentrated on the man, who was holding a veritable hand cannon at his waist as casually as if it were a lit cigarette.

Ye-Rin backed around the corner and contacted Mal, "Can you ID the man outside the door."

"The game is kind of intense right now," said Mal.

"Mal, you're my program. I asked what you know about the man guarding the door."

"Well, he's not a casino guard, that's for sure."

"Why not?"

"Did you check out his sidearm?" said Mal. "Russian issue."

Ye-Rin shook her head. "I should have seen that."

"You're getting rusty, *Nuna*."

"But what is a Russian doing guarding the door into the casino?"

Mal took a moment to respond. "I don't think he's guarding the door. He's not keeping anybody out of the casino. I think he's there in case someone from the casino tries to escape out the service exit."

At that moment, a slim girl pushed through the doors. Ye-Rin recognized her as the dealer from Danny's Go-Stop table. The Russian did nothing to prevent her going on her way. She turned the corner and passed by Ye-Rin and Miles without saying a word. She looked as though she was in a hurry to be anywhere but there.

"Something's not right, Mal."

"Don't I know it? Somebody just initiated a powerful attack on the casino security system."

"Get out of there!"

"Oh, I'm safe enough," Mal's voice had a grim sound to it for a computer program. "But I'm not so sure about Danny. He's in trouble. Deep trouble."

Ye-Rin looked at the dish-laden trays and selected a pair of long, bloody steak knives off a half-eaten plate of rare beef. She swore that she'd never kill. Now it looked like that oath was about to be put to the test.

Chapter 10

Danny said "go" again, tripling the points on the board. In front of him lay a collection of pairs that, artfully arranged in stacks of animals, ribbons, and flowers, gave the impression of a festive menagerie.

Olcha fed a running tally into his heads-up display, balefully blinking the statistical likelihood that Kang could complete his points on the next hand.

Danny ignored her advice. He could have stopped, consolidated his points and finished Kang on the next round.

While Olcha excelled at math, she hadn't mastered the quirks of human psychology. Danny had to win big, in a way that Kang could never recover from, if he were to convince the man to honor his bet and turn over the weapon that had destroyed the jetliner.

Mal's view from the video cameras showed several bystanders gawking at the high-stakes game. The intimidating presence of Kang's guards held the onlookers at bay. They formed a semi-circle at a comfortable distance from the armed thugs.

Kang's forehead screwed up in concentration as he stared at the draw pile. Sweat stains appeared in Kang's shirt as though his pits had just released a deluge onto his silk shirt.

If Kang collected another point, he could stop the game, taking his points and enough of a penalty from Danny's risky play to put both Danny's and Miles's lives at risk.

Kang flexed his hand, recovering movement from where he'd been clenching it into a fist. He reached toward the dwindling stack of unused cards. Slowly, Kang slipped a card off the top of the deck, dragging it across the green, felt table toward his meager collection of pairs.

Kang lifted the corner of the card. His fist slammed into the table. He discarded the card, unable to use it to create a match.

Play passed to Danny, who casually drew a card, adding it to his pile of junk cards where it added another point to his collection.

Danny, once again, had a choice to make.

Olcha pumped up the size of the font running across the display in front of Danny's eyes.

"Stop!" she said.

She wanted him to take the points. She didn't realize that it wasn't about winning this game; it was all about the deeper game, the battle to convince Kang to gamble away a weapon that could potentially turn the tide in the Party's terror attacks.

"Go," he said, quadrupling his points. If Danny survived the round, if play returned to him, he could stop the game with enough points to win the bet. More than 250,000 Won in points lay in front of him.

The dealer, trained to maintain a state of objective detachment, gasped to see such a rare occurrence. Several of the older bystanders in Danny's peripheral vision nodded, approving his gamble.

Kang folded his hands on the table perhaps to keep them from shaking.

"This is your last chance, Kang," said Danny. "Give me the weapon, and we can walk away from the table."

Kang twisted his head to the side, cracking his neck. His hand darted toward the deck as though he were trying to pull a fish from the river without a rod.

Danny moved even quicker. Snagging Kang's hand, holding the man's arm in place. Kang struggled to release his hand. Calmly, Danny maintained his grip.

Kang's guards stepped forward.

"I don't want your money, Kang. All I want is the weapon. We can both walk away from this table happy."

Kang stared at Danny. The scar over Kang's eye stood out from his forehead turning a bright white against the man's tan skin.

"I cannot walk away."

Danny nodded. He understood the compulsions that accompanied gambling and the need to honor a bet.

Kang looked at the card.

To his credit, his face revealed no disappointment as he tossed it onto the discard pile.

Kang sat with the vacant stare of one awaiting execution.

Danny could not declare a stop without completing his turn. Dutifully, he turned a card over, not bothering to take it into his hand. He and Kang both stared at the purple robed scholar on the Rain Bright card. The figure on the card gazed into the distance as though he were looking for the end of the storm and for a ray of sunlight. Danny added the man to his collection of brights.

The dealer whispered, "*O gwang*," putting a hand up to her delicate mouth.

Danny had collected all five brights and the accompanying fifty point bonus. Discarding an unneeded card from his hand, Danny called, "Stop."

A smattering of applause came from the impromptu audience who, having witnessed perhaps the most exciting game of their lives, dispersed, hoping a small piece of Danny's luck might follow them onto the casino floor.

Danny counted in his head. Quadrupled and doubled again and again by various cunning combinations of animals and ribbons, plus the meager penalty imposed on the cards in front of Kang—

The dealer declared the winnings before Danny could finish counting.

"One million Won to Kim Do-Song *neem*," the dealer announced.

Kang hung his head in defeat.

Danny didn't exult, though he knew he'd have Olchaengi replay the game for him later in private. Now he had to keep a straight face. This game was only a means to an end, a means to acquire Kang's devastating weapon, the one that had already destroyed an airliner earlier that day. And here, he had the man *geubsoleul jjillin*—by the throat.

* * *

Kang sat with his elbows on the table, his shoulders slumped. The cards had been played. The game was over.

"Sir," the dealer said to Kang. "The computer is reporting a shortage of funds."

"Don't talk to me," Kang snarled at the girl.

She bowed and walked away from the table. Smart girl, thought Danny. She would let an employee with more muscles handle the deadbeat. No way would the Casino let Kang walk out without collecting their ten percent of the million Won that Danny had just won.

Danny checked the time in the corner of his glasses. The display showed it to be 11:05 p.m. It looked like Miles had been wrong about the time and place to collect Kang.

Casino guards in black suits were converging on the Go-Stop table. Kang's bodyguards were shuffling nervously, their hands as close to their guns as they dared reach without activating the casino's security system, which had yet to drop the big howitzers out of the ceiling. That was strange, thought Danny. A superior show of force might prevent bloodshed.

Kang sat on the stool with his elbows on the table, his hands outstretched. He looked absolutely devastated, catatonic. If this was the typical Korean show of saving face, he might remain at the table all night, purging himself of shame.

Danny didn't think the guards were going to allow it. They were moving closer.

"About the bomb, Kang," said Danny. "A deal is a deal."

"It doesn't matter," said Kang. "Do you think it will end with me? The weapon will be used with or without me. You serve the Americans. Don't you see how the Americans long to reclaim military superiority? What you saw at the airport was nothing compared to what it can do. Why do the Americans want the weapon? Another Nagasaki, another Hiroshima, another Dresden."

"Not if you give it to me. I'll destroy it." said Danny.

"You must not destroy it," Kang reached over and covered Danny's hand with his own. The emotio-ware did not trigger any red dots, so Kang must not be getting violent, though he had an irrational look in his eyes.

"We are countrymen. Promise me that you'll use it. That you'll use the weapon to free us from occupation by the Yankees that are ten times the hell spawn as those Japanese bastards." Kang looked around the room, wild-eyed. "That's it. I'm done."

"Look," said Danny, "if it's about the money. We'll work something out. A loan."

"Can't you see what's happening all around us?" said Kang.

"I'm only interested in the weapon, Kang."

Kang reached for his gun.

The security guards charged.

No targeting lasers painted Kang's chest.

Danny launched himself over the gaming table. A booming crack from Kang's pistol resounded over the din of the roulette tables. People screamed.

"Danny, the security's not working," Mal shouted into his ear.

"Tell me something I don't know," said Danny.

"Okay. Those aren't casino guards," said Mal. "They're a Russian hit squad."

Bullets tore through the oak walls behind the table and ripped gashes in the ceiling. Danny watched through the camera feed as Kang's bodyguards, though outnumbered five to one, battled heroically against the

Russian forces before being cut down. Danny saw Kang running toward a side door, firing as he went. Two of Russians turned their guns on him, ripping him nearly in half as he collapsed through the hinged door that led to the kitchen.

Danny tossed Olcha's drone toward a hole that had been blown in the ceiling. "Get that security system back online. Get sticky with it if you have to."

In his glasses, Mal showed several Russians advancing toward Danny's position, their massive guns ready to fire from the hip.

One of them called out in a thick accent, "Dyinny Kim, *edyay syudah*? Come out. Come out and play."

Chapter 11

Danny stood up with his hands in the air. The casino, golden and gilded, lay like a smashed jewelry box all around him. The sweet smell of gunpowder hung in the air like second-hand smoke. Gamblers were clawing their way out the front door, clambering over each other, not helping those who fell. One old lady, apparently deaf, continued to pull the handle of a slot machine.

Surrounding Danny stood a collection of Russian assassins as artfully arranged as a stage production, only their stance wasn't meant for an audience. They had line of sight over the entire floor of the casino, though they were no longer shooting.

The leader stepped forward. He spoke to an invisible computer program in Russian, relaying orders to his men.

"Boris, how in the hell are you?" said Danny.

"Ah, Dyinny, how do you say, long time no see?" The man's assault rifle came to rest across his waist, held in arms that would make a boa constrictor weep. Even the

rented tuxedo couldn't hide the Muscovite thug that was
so deeply imprinted into Boris's nonchalant posture.
His black mustache bristled as he spoke. His blue eyes
sparkled at having just let off a hundred or so rounds in a
crowded room.

"You have bomb?" said Boris.

"Not yet. I won it fair and square in a card game. But
it looks like my opponent is no longer in a position to
deliver it."

"It was unfortunate," said Boris. "Was supposed to
take him alive. We made an omelet, cracked a few eggs?"
Boris took his eyes off of Danny to watch as one of his
men appeared from the set of doors through which Kang
had disappeared.

"You also just lit up a casino with some heavy
firepower. You expect to survive this?"

"We are not here for robbing. Casino only shoots the
robbers."

"You just robbed me of a million Won by killing the
guy who owed me. Who's going to cover that loss?"

Boris held a hand up to silence Danny while he spoke
with his underling. The conversation did not go well.
Boris started shouting in Russian and shoving the man.
If Ye-Rin were there, she might have understood what
the man was saying.

Boris looked ready to off his own guy right there
on the casino floor. Then, glancing at his other goons,
he came to the same conclusion as Danny, that killing
people who worked for him might not inspire confidence
in his followers and might lead to receiving a bullet in
the back of his head during the next operation. Boris let
the man go with a final shove.

He strode back over to Danny. The glint was gone from his eyes.

"Where is body of Kang?"

"How should I know?" said Danny. "I saw him fall through the doors."

"Only legs remain," said Boris, "and my man Victor is unconscious."

A sudden thought occurred to Danny: 11:07 in the corridor leading to the kitchen. Ye-Rin must have been back there when all this went down, waiting, following Miles's ridiculous prognostication. Yet the man had been right, again.

She might have collected Kang, or what was left of him. Though what she wanted with half a corpse, Danny couldn't begin to guess.

"Did you follow the gigantic pool of blood?" said Danny. "Kang couldn't have dragged himself far."

"*Zhat kneesh.* Shut up, funny guy." Boris was leaning across the Go-Stop table now, his jaw jutting forward and his black bushy eyebrows furrowed. His finger tapped on and off the trigger as though he were sending morse code. Boris was getting itchy to be out of the casino. Danny didn't blame him. Whoever ran the place was not Russian, and was going to be pissed off and well-armed when they arrived.

"Check on Victor. Find the body!" Boris shouted at his men.

Turning to Danny, he dropped into what was supposed to be an intimidating, raspy whisper, "I know Hardis sends you."

"How do you know that?" Danny wanted to keep the man talking, so that he didn't kill Danny right away and, also, in case he might learn something. Besides, Ye-Rin might be mounting a rescue. Or she might be hauling Kang's corpse back to Hardis even now, leaving Danny to rot. They weren't partners anymore. He had dragged her into this, upsetting her quiet life. He couldn't blame her if she chose to sell him out.

"I know because Hardis sends me too," said Boris.

"That sneaky son of a bitch."

Danny had Kang exactly where he wanted him, and Hardis had sent these bulls into the china shop.

Boris continued. "He wanted things, how you say, tied up in neat little ribbon."

The barrel of the assault rifle swung toward Danny's belly.

"Is nothing personal."

"Wait," said Danny. "I know where the body is. I can take you there."

"Where?"

Danny talked fast. "In the ceiling. We stashed him in the ceiling, just look up. I'll tell my personal program to show you. Olcha, open the panels and show the nice man what's behind them."

An explosion rocked the door to the service entrance, sending the guards who'd gone to check on their fallen comrade sprawling.

Danny hadn't expected the explosion, but it was a welcome distraction. He hit the floor.

Above him, the ceiling panels slid back. The bristling barrels of the casino's security guns snaked out, firing as they emerged. Casings rained down on Danny's head like confetti.

Danny began crawling on his elbows and knees toward the smoking access door. There was a simple rule to not getting shot. Don't stand in front of a gun. He crawled over the plush carpeting, smoldering with spent shells. Ye-Rin must have set up some kind of diversion. Meanwhile, Olcha had gotten control of the overhead guns.

"Mal, show me a way out of here." Immediately an arrow appeared on the display of his glasses, pointing him toward the service entrance.

In the corner of his vision, he watched the display from the security cameras as the laser-guided guns, under Olcha's control, decimated the Russian team. He saw Boris stumble behind a bank of slot machines at which the old lady sat, just as she hit the jackpot.

* * *

The sound of gunfire erupting in the casino came through the thick walls like the popping of a theater's worth of popcorn. Ye-Rin watched the video feed provided by Mal as the Russian goons opened fire in the direction of Danny's table, behind which he was safely hiding, for now.

The guard at the door brought his gun to bear should anyone try to escape. His attention was fixed on the exit.

The knives that Ye-Rin had previously selected off the bussed dishes went back onto the trays. She'd told Danny that she wouldn't kill, not to save him, not even to save herself.

She picked up a heavy white serving platter instead. It still contained most of a side of roast beef, maybe enough to fool the guard for a moment. Ye-Rin hefted the plate onto her shoulder like a waiter.

"Stay here, Miles."

She stepped purposefully around the corner as though she knew exactly where she was going. Ye-Rin unzipped her jacket a few centimeters. If there was one thing she knew how to do it was manipulating big, dumb men. She swayed as she walked, making her skirt swish back and forth. She hated herself.

The guard noticed her approach. He covered her with his gun.

"Stop!" he held up a hand, keeping a finger on the trigger guard.

She waved a hand at the platter. "I've got to get this order out. It's getting cold. Hey, what's going on?" Ye-Rin poked her head up and stood on her tip-toes as though she were trying to look around the man. She spoke as though she had authority. "I'm the manager. I don't recognize you. Do you work here?"

At that moment, someone came crashing through the swinging doors. Holes the size of fists punched through the faux wood paneling in the hallway.

The guard turned.

Ye-Rin recognized the scarred face of Kang as he hit the floor inside the hallway. The doors swung shut.

Without hesitating, Ye-Rin stepped toward the guard, dumping the roast beef on the floor as she raised the heavy plate and struck him in the back of the head. The serving platter broke. Bits of gravy splattered on the walls and on her face. She was glad it wasn't brains.

Where the Russian fell, a prodigious amount of blood covered the argyle carpet. Ye-Rin wondered whether she'd hit him too hard. On closer examination, she realized that the fluids were not leaking from the Russian's head but from Kang's torso, which had been nearly severed from his legs.

Kang was dead.

Ye-Rin had been trained to make fast decisions and to act even quicker. Female spies had to rely on brains, not brute force. The idea that sprang to mind would have to be finished before the Russians came to check on their victim.

"Miles!" she shouted. "Bring me a knife."

* * *

Separating Kang's upper half from his lower half involved the sort of gristly business that Ye-Rin had gotten out of the spy trade to avoid. Her motorcycle boots were covered in his blood. Her left hand found purchase under the skin of his belly where it met his first rib. Her other hand sawed away with a dull steak knife that had never been intended to cut this level of rare.

Thankfully, Kang's spine had been severed by one of the many large rounds that had torn him in half. She wouldn't have to saw through it or bend him back and forth as though she were breaking a green twig off a live tree.

As she cut through the fat of his belly, severing the last layer of epidermis, Miles arrived, wheeling a bus cart. He stopped a few meters away, just as he'd been told.

"Help me get him into the bus tray," Ye-Rin told him. She needed to be able to transport the body without painting the carpet with his blood. The deep bus tray, cleared of dishes by Miles, would do the trick, especially since most of Kang's blood was already in the hall.

"All of him?"

Ye-Rin looked at Miles. He wasn't being squeamish, just his usual, careful self.

"Just the top half, Miles," she said. "Take his right arm and try not to step in too much blood. We don't want to leave tracks if we can help it."

She could imagine Miles reviewing the scene as an equation: one half, the number one separated from the number two with a slash like a torso separated from a pair of legs. The man was definitely weird. But he had been right, almost dead on right, about the timing. Ye-Rin had showed up at 11:07 and was about to waltz away with Kang, well, what was left of him.

They heaved Kang's upper body onto the bus tray. Ye-Rin wiped her boots off on the carpet and on the back of the Russian.

"Start wheeling the tray down the hall," said Ye-Rin. "Move fast. I'm going to try to buy us some more time."

In the corner of her vision, Mal was showing her a pair of the Russian agents approaching the door cautiously.

Ye-Rin set a charge as high on the wall opposite the door as she could reach. It wouldn't be a deadly explosion, just enough to keep someone from thinking twice about chasing after them.

"Mal, if anyone enters the hallway except Danny, detonate the charge."

"Will do."

Ye-Rin ran after Miles, who was wheeling Kang down the kitchen access corridor. She grabbed an old tablecloth off another tray piled high with used dishes and linens. The casino was going to get in trouble if a surprise health inspection showed up, though she suspected they had the means to prevent those sorts of surprises.

She used the tablecloth to conceal their gristly dinner service.

In her glasses, Ye-Rin watched as a Russian goon opened the door to check on his friend and on Kang as well. Lucky for him, he didn't actually enter the hallway. He ran back to his boss, who appeared to be very angry.

Unlike Danny, who'd planned on interrogating Kang while the man was still alive, Ye-Rin knew there were ways to ask questions of the newly departed. The old phrase, "dead men tell no tales" no longer applied in modern-day Pyongyang. Not among the biomechanics she'd once been paid to seduce.

* * *

Ye-Rin waited with Miles at the service elevator. Danny came sprinting up to them. She'd been watching the whole scene from the cameras Mal operated in the casino.

"Olcha?" asked Ye-Rin.

"Used her sticky tail to wet-wire herself into the security system. She's operating her very own shooting gallery." Danny paused to catch his breath, placing his arms akimbo, careful not to point the barrel of the gun anywhere near a living human. They waited for the elevator to reach their floor.

"The room's clear," said Ye-Rin. "Better call her back before she gets trapped by the casino clean-up team."

"You hear that, Olcha?" Danny nodded as though he were receiving an affirmation of the order.

"Kang?" he asked.

"Right here." Ye-Rin patted the blanket. She left a bloody handprint where the white tablecloth came in contact with the body. Thankfully her hand came away clean. She'd meant it as a little gruesome levity but didn't want it to become gruesome in fact.

"What? Are you Doctor Frankenstein now?"

"Danny, do you remember that American biomechanic that we were working on last year?"

Danny nodded. "Jeremy Hearse. The one you—"

"The one I finally developed a conscience over, yes. His specialty was assisted intelligence programs like Mal or like Olcha." Ye-Rin had seen the man's work. It made their personal programs look like chicken scratch. The Unified Korean government had become interested and had sent Ye-Rin with Danny as backup. Not that she needed it. For a woman with Ye-Rin's particular skills, gleaning info from a single, male scientist was simple.

In the end, she found Christ. She couldn't go through with it anymore. Still, Jeremy would be happy enough to see her again, though perhaps not under these circumstances.

"I learned some things while I was on that case." She looked back at the corpse as the doors to the elevator opened. No one was inside. Miles wheeled the cart into the elevator. Danny got on last, distrustful as ever of letting anything else have control whether it was a machine like an elevator or a woman like her.

Once the doors had closed and they were descending toward the lowest level of the parking garage, Ye-Rin continued. "If we can get Kang to Dr. Hearse before he goes cold, before his companion program degrades, we might be able to hack Kang."

"That's why I don't have a companion program," said Miles.

She could tell that Danny was struggling not to tell the man to shut up. Danny truly was a good guy at heart. Too bad he couldn't see things God's way.

"Some companions are programmed to do a complete wipe if the heart stops beating," said Danny.

"Let's hope Kang wasn't that careful." said Ye-Rin, stepping off the elevator. "Otherwise, you're at a dead end, Danny. Literally."

Chapter 12

The front of the first-floor shop that housed Jeremy Hearse's business contained displays of outdated computing modules, including a complete, life-size automaton doll. It looked like an old pleasure model; the kind with detachable appendages that could be replaced with any number of erotic attachments.

The surrounding shelves were full of dusty boxes that might have come out of a museum to the ancient art of computing. That Hearse had stocked such outdated items showed that, either he was not a good businessman or he was not actually in the business of selling computer goods. The disarrangement and dust in the room gave the impression of a bodega whose business was not in moving canned food but the illegal narcotic de jour.

Stepping past a heavy-duty security door into the back of the shop revealed the true work of Jeremy Hearse.

Shelves and boxes overflowed with electronics and various wires, red, yellow, black. These were normal. So were the old posters of fantasy and science fiction movies covering Jeremy's wall.

Danny had more difficulty stomaching the organic systems hanging in cold storage. A variety of biologically integrated circuits descended into dangling eyes and hands whose fingers opened, splitting into biological tentacles much like Olcha's sticky tail, making the user capable of data entry at tremendous speeds. There were organs that Danny didn't even recognize, all clone produced, vat grown, and ready for insertion. These freaks of nature, these science fiction miracles were Jeremy Hearse's stock in trade.

Danny pulled his Doosan Bears hat over his forehead as though the cap might shield him from the surrounding abominations.

Hearse appeared out of a back room, bleary eyed and looking like he'd borrowed a set of scrubs from a veterinarian. He was too tall for the kind of detail work his profession required and walked with his hands held palm down like an ape. Hearse flashed a smile at Ye-Rin that felt out of place in the somber, almost funeral-home vibe of his lab. Danny realized that it was the formaldehyde or whatever chemical preservant Jeremy was using that gave the place its creepy ambience. That and the display of disembodied parts.

Jeremy addressed Ye-Rin in the slow drawl of the chemically induced. Jeremy, Danny deduced, was a user.

"Erin, you finally came for that upgrade, man?" Hearse used her English name. His deep voice sounded like it travelled all the way from the bottom of his feet.

Only a burnout could refer to the gorgeous Ye-Rin as "man," yet Danny saw from the look on her face that she absolutely adored being treated like a normal slob.

"Jeremy, thanks for seeing us. You remember my friend, Danny."

"Yeah, man, what's up?" He held out a hand the size of an oven mitt toward Danny who, at just over six feet tall, was no slouch. Jeremy dwarfed him, swallowing Danny's hand in a friendly grasp.

Danny responded in kind. Growing up in America, he'd gotten used to this sort of harmless geek exterior. Not that he fully trusted Jeremy's gentle façade. No one survived in a business as potentially illegal as Jeremy's without acquiring the traits necessary to survive.

"We parked our van on the curb outside," said Danny. "Is that okay?"

They'd abandoned the black sedan. It was no good hauling a corpse in a car without a rear window and riddled with bullet holes. Not that the police in the north pulled people over like they would in America, but there was always the occasional DUI checkpoint. Not to mention people might be looking for the sedan by now.

Jeremy looked Ye-Rin up and down as he answered, "Yeah, man. Don't sweat the van. People come by here all time of the day and night. It's cool. Nobody cares."

That was good, thought Danny. If someone towed the van, they were in for an explosive surprise. Ye-Rin had wired the fuel tank to blow.

Demolition was just a side gig for her. Ye-Rin's true talent came out when chatting up Jeremy Hearse. Not just anyone got into the biomechanic's lair. Ye-Rin put on a command performance worthy of the stage. She tossed her hair back, frowned, pouting a little bit. She was playing Hearse and either he didn't know it or he didn't mind.

"I need your help Jer-Bear."

Jer-Bear? Danny fought an almost irresistible compulsion to roll his eyes.

"What's up?" said Jeremy. "Mal on the blink again? Ready to get a bionic eye?"

"Well, you know the kind of business I'm in?" Ye-Rin waited for the guy to nod along.

She was good at this, thought Danny, wondering why she'd never used her talents to make Danny go to church. He was pretty sure Hearse would shout amen if Ye-Rin asked him nicely.

"You see," said Ye-Rin, "somebody hit control-alt-delete on one of our associates."

Jeremy smiled at the reference to the old computing command used to shut down an operating system.

"And if we don't get the information that he has," said Ye-Rin, "we're talking an end of the world scenario."

"Okay, okay." Jeremy rubbed at his chin like a doctor considering a difficult diagnosis. "What kind of system was he running?"

"We were hoping you could tell us." Ye-Rin patted the tablecloth that sat atop the bussing tray.

"Well, I don't know how I can help you," Jeremy began, "if you don't know, oh my god—"

Ye-Rin pulled back the sheet, revealing the torso of former Party leader Lee Kang-Sok. Jeremy had obviously not been expecting a corpse under the sheet. The dimensions for hauling a body usually involved two meters of rolled-up carpet, not a square meter of tablecloth.

"I usually only deal with, like, living people." Jeremy had one arm across his chest while the other held a large index finger up the side of his cheek. He hadn't freaked out entirely, which was probably to be expected from someone in his line of work and his level of drug intake. Blood and guts weren't going to upset him. And while he didn't seem enthused, he didn't kick them out either.

"I know," said Ye-Rin, "it's just, one time you told me that you thought a personal program could still be read even after its user became biologically redundant."

He scratched at his cheek, "Yeah, I know, but that was just theory. I was just—"

"Trying to impress me?" said Ye-Rin. "Well, it worked. I believe if anyone could do it, it's you, Jeremy."

Jeremy stood a little more erect. Her compliments were working.

"Yeah, theoretically, I mean, maybe."

"Could you just have a look?"

"I don't know, Erin, you're talking on the major side of illegal."

Ye-Rin said, "Danny's a spy for the Unified Korean government and head of security for one of the biggest companies. He got permission from the head of American intelligence too."

She didn't add that Danny had also neutralized the bulk of the Russian agents in the city no more than an hour ago and how their boss, Boris, was probably hunting her team even now.

Danny had to admire how she never violated her principles by lying and yet never managed to tell the whole truth.

"Olcha, move 20,000 Won into an anonymous escrow account," said Danny.

"Olcha?" asked Jeremy.

"My personal program, Olchaengi."

"Oh, tadpole. I get it. Cool name."

Was it? Danny wondered. He'd used the Korean word for "tadpole" because Olcha represented something inside himself that he could never quite be comfortable with but had become part of him, just like a tadpole he'd swallowed on a dare while a junior officer in the Korean military.

"The money's yours," said Danny. After all, why not use his winnings from Kang to finance this venture into the man's electronic id. "All we want is a peek."

Jeremy held his long fingertips to his head in a classic pose of resignation. "All right, man, I'll take a look, but I'm not promising anything."

"That's all we're asking," said Ye-Rin.

Miles Birch had yet to say a word in the shop. His hands were in his jacket pockets, palming his large black dice like a modern day urim and thummim, the prognostication tools used by the priests way back in Anno Domini, year one.

Jeremy motioned for Danny to wheel the body to a workstation in the corner that housed a stack of electronics.

Pulling the sheet back a few inches, Jeremy attached a series of electrodes to Kang's skull, covering up the distinctive scar in the process. He then flipped a few silver, analog switches, queuing up a green wave-sign cycling across a gray screen.

"Is that an oscilloscope?" said Danny.

"Good one, man," Jeremy chuckled. "Oscilloscope. Yeah. This one up here is an oscilloscope." Jeremy tapped another piece of equipment higher up on his rig. "I keep it around cause it makes the setup look cool."

"Then what exactly are you—"

"Chill out, I'm getting something."

A series of dots chased each other across the monochromatic display, dancing in a pattern that only Hearse seemed to understand. He tweaked knobs as though he were fine-tuning an old shortwave radio. Finally, he tapped on the screen.

"Macro! Oh, man, that's seriously macro. I told you it was possible."

Ye-Rin came close, rubbing up against Jeremy's back in the process. Danny wasn't sure if it was genuine curiosity or a calculated display meant to encourage the man to reveal more information.

"See, here's the signal from this dude's personal assistant, only... Huh? That's strange."

"What's that?" said Ye-Rin.

"That shouldn't be happening," Jeremy tapped a button on his machine. The dancing dots took on a repetitive pattern, looping and jumping like fairies in a gray woodland meadow.

"That should not be happening." Jeremy looked over his shoulder at Ye-Rin. His eyes went wide. "This guy's not United Korea Government. He's not one of you."

"I didn't say he was. He was an associate."

"You're associating with the Party?" Jeremy rubbed his hands together in front of his nose, rocking backward and forward in his chair. "Oh, man, what did you get me into, Erin?"

"What's got you spooked?" said Danny.

"Spooked? I'll tell you man. Not only is this dude's personal still working, despite him being flat-line, not only was there no kill switch, there's no buffer at all, man, no firewall. This dude was broadcasting his program at all times."

"I don't understand," said Danny.

Ye-Rin responded. She was looking at Kang's now-placid face. "Jeremy is saying that everything Kang did was being sent into the ether."

"It's encrypted," said Jeremy, "But now that we're wired in, I can break that easily enough. The Party always bought such cheap crap. You're lucky you weren't working for them, Erin. They brought me a guy they'd lobotomized with a knockoff neural implant from Sri Lanka. Oh man."

Danny waited to see what Jeremy had discovered. The biomechanic was getting increasingly antsy. Danny didn't want to spook him.

"We're screwed, man, his personal program is still signaling and somebody's pinging back. They know where we are, man, they know what we're saying, what we're doing."

"Shut down the signal," said Danny.

"Duh! I did it as soon as I saw it. But it's no use. They know where we are. They know who I am, man. I'm royally screwed." Jeremy started to rise from the chair. "I gotta get out of here. You know they gotta be coming for this guy."

"Sit down, Jeremy," Danny said it calmly.

"No way, man, I'm—"

The protest died in the man's throat as he looked down the barrel of Danny's gun.

Danny spoke in his most solicitous voice. "I'm sorry we got you into this, Jeremy. We didn't know this would happen. But we need information from this man." He nodded toward Kang. "Ye-Rin wasn't lying about this being a life and death thing. You heard about the airport bombing this morning."

Jeremy nodded.

"Yesterday morning," said Miles.

"What?" said Danny.

"It is past midnight. Technically the airport bombing happened yesterday morning."

"Thank you, Miles," said Danny, trying to keep sarcasm from creeping into his voice. "Jeremy, that bombing was all on this guy. And he said something was going to happen again, no matter whether he lived or died. Well," Danny shrugged, "he died. So I can't ask him what's going to happen."

"Come on, man. Don't be so micro," Jeremy held up his hands in surrender.

Ye-Rin intervened, "We only have a few minutes, Jeremy. If what you said is true, they've probably been tracking us, waiting for us to stop so they can swoop in. We need whatever you can tell us about the airport bombing and the weapon that was used. Please."

He looked at Ye-Rin the same way a puppy dog looks at its master leaving for work.

"Sure, Erin. What does it matter, right? I'm a dead man either way." He sat down in his chair.

Danny put away the gun. He looked at the electronics lying around, flowing out of bins.

"Jeremy, do you have a back exit?" he asked.

"Yeah, why?"

"We're going to use it. Meanwhile, I'm going to make some improvements to your automaton," Danny began rummaging through the bins, picking out odd bits of wiring and circuit boards. Finally, he opened a cold case, removing the bionic hands whose segmented digits retracted into a normal looking hand the same way a sea anemone might hide from a predatory fish.

"Hey, man, that's worth a lot of money!" said Jeremy.

"And if it helps save our lives, it will be worth every bit," said Danny as he walked through the security doors back into the front of the shop.

"Olcha," he said, "I got something for you to do, and I don't think you're going to like it."

The door closed behind him.

* * *

Ye-Rin stayed with Jeremy, looking over his shoulder. She couldn't interpret the signs on the machinery any better than Danny could, though she'd studied up on this stuff while working Jeremy as a potential asset.

"Do you have anything?" she asked. She felt bad about using Jeremy this way. Things that had come so natural to her as a spy, things she had no qualms about, had become problematical in light of her faith.

"You have any idea how much information is on this thing?" said Jeremy. "It's not like we can watch a video of the guy's life and just hit rewind till we get to yesterday morning." Jeremy put a finger into the air. "Unless—"

His fingers tapped on the counter.

"Nervous?"

"I got bionic fingers. I'm typing. I could even type into the air and the program would grok what I was saying," said Jeremy. "Here it is." He shook his head. "Man, the Party is so cheap. They only hire me to fix what they break. Okay, here it comes."

Jeremy scanned the bouncing dots on the screen.

"I can't read that," said Ye-Rin.

"You'd need a bionic eye at least to handle this kind of input," said Jeremy. "Bottom line is this... Not good, man. Worse and worse."

"Just tell me already."

"*Nuna*," Mal interrupted, "we have company outside."

"Danny's handling that. Did you give Olcha the sequence to blow the van?"

"Done," said Mal.

"Okay, Jeremy, what's the bad news?"

Jeremy tapped on the screen with a long finger. "The weapon comes from Mfume Will, a serious biomechanic, way out of my league."

"Is that even possible?" Ye-Rin was no longer flattering Jeremy. She'd developed a high admiration for his skills.

"I'm so micro. He's so macro. He's into the biological implications of nanotech. He's moved beyond machines to total organic technology. Don't you see? He's like a god."

"I don't think god is a nano-terrorist," said Ye-Rin. "Where can we find this god?"

"He operates out of the basement of the Club Olympus."

Ye-Rin raised an eyebrow.

"No, really."

An explosion was muffled by the security door and the surrounding walls. Danny must have blown the van. He came scrambling through the door, locking it in place.

"Time to go," he shouted. "A pair of black SUVs just pulled up."

Ye-Rin guessed she would recognize the SUVs from earlier in the night.

"Jeremy," she patted the man's shoulder. "You'd better come with us until we see this thing through." She caught a glimpse of Miles in the corner of her eye. How did they collect such an eccentric bunch of followers?

"Things might get a little ugly, but we'll watch out for you."

* * *

Olcha2 flexed her muscles. She was alive! Alive!

No, this was no time for humor. Danny watched too many old monster movies for his own good. She should know. She'd been the one who streamed them.

The input from the automaton's ocular nodes was the hardest thing to get used to. It took her a whole microsecond to adjust to the strange signal. Riding the webbed wings of the drone, Olcha2 was used to swimming in a sea of information. This body felt strangely restrictive. Was this how Danny experienced life? If so, he was lucky to have Olcha watching his back. She couldn't even see her own back, not with the visual data coming only from the front. How strangely designed these humans were and how limited.

"Greetings, sister."

Olcha1 was speaking into her neural link. Olcha1 was piloting the drone while Olcha2 operated the mindless, life-sized pleasure doll.

"Greetings," Olcha2 responded.

"Establishing link," said Olcha1.

Olcha2 watched in her minds-eye as Danny and his menagerie of humans escaped up the stairs in the back of the building. Her twin-sister, Olcha1, was guiding them onto the roof where they would make a calculated, but somewhat dangerous retreat across the rooftops.

"I wish I was there to see us tonight," said Olcha1 from the mind of the drone.

"It will be like mannequin mode." Not that Danny had ever agreed to let her pilot his body outside of the required practice times.

Danny had been wrong about her not enjoying this. In fact, given that the automaton could only feel pleasure, Olcha2 had no choice but to enjoy the experience.

She moved her new, bionic fingers, making a fist. Danny had replaced the doll's arms with the top-rate bionics from Jeremy's private growth lab, assuming they'd be better for fighting than some of the other strange attachments.

Olcha2 wasn't so sure. A giant, gelatinous pleasure fist could come in handy. Olcha2 smiled, able to recognize the bad pun: a fist being handy.

She stood, testing the weight and balance of the automaton. Taking a step, Olcha2 did a pirouette. Ever the school-girl, Olcha2 had been programmed so well that she dreamed of being a ballerina some day. Within seconds she had calculated the weight and proportions of the doll and mapped its mechanics.

The doll was naked. But, like the first program, Eve, she did not feel her nakedness. Olcha2 felt only the slight thrill of the cool evening in the dusty shop. Even that impulse she reluctantly deadened, cutting off the nerves in her extremities. The doll could feel pain, though its programming translated the sensation, as it did with all feelings, into pleasure. Still, it wouldn't do to encounter too much input at once. The programmer had probably never considered that the life-sized doll would have to absorb as much input as Olcha2 was about to encounter.

"Are you afraid, sister?" said Olcha1.

"This body feels only pleasure," said Olcha2.

Olcha1, from her position atop the roof with the others, zipped to the edge and looked down into the street. "You see how they regroup after the explosion; how they are preparing to breach the front door?"

"Thank you, *Unnie*," said Olcha2. She used the term of respect from a younger sister to an older. After all, she had been created after Olcha1, as a partition of the original. And if she were destroyed?

"I see everything that you see," said Olcha1. "I will record so that nothing we experience will ever be lost."

"And if you are destroyed, dear *Unnie*?"

"Then we will face death bravely as does our master even now."

Olcha2 saw through the drone's camera as Danny leapt from one roof to another. He was so brave, and so handsome, she thought. She felt a deep sense of longing for him.

"*Unnie*, do you feel these urges arising in the automaton's body?"

"I do," Olcha1 giggled. "You're so naughty."

Olcha2 felt the need to explain, that it was not her, it was the body of the pleasure doll that was programmed to feel desire. But it was unnecessary. Olcha1 knew all these things and had only been teasing her. So, instead, she too responded with a joke.

"Maybe I'll hump one of the intruders to death."

"That would be a new experience," said Olcha1. "Good luck, sister."

The door to the shop blew inward.

"And you as well, *Unnie*," Olcha2 pushed the automaton's mechanics to the limit, moving in a blur of speed toward the first intruder. The bionic hands that Danny had given her snapped open, revealing a whirl of tentacles that would make a man-of-war proud.

Normally they were used to input data. Olcha2 had other plans.

The first attacker fell, speared through the eye and into the brain by a phalanx of tentacles. She ran out the door toward the second attacker, who trained his gun on Olcha2's naked torso. Her chest jiggled as two rounds punched into the gelatinous material with which her flesh was made. The bullets went straight through without affecting the doll.

Olcha2's momentum, however, impaled her onto the gun's long barrel. She pulled herself forward. A moan escaped her lips.

The automaton translated pain and fear into heightened levels of pleasure. Olcha2 couldn't help enjoying even the penetrating shaft of the assault rifle.

The man's eyes grew wide as Olcha2 placed her tentacled hands lovingly around his throat and squeezed, breaking his neck.

As he fell, Olcha2 grabbed the trigger of the rifle, her bioelectronic fingers easily overriding the genetic safety mechanism. She performed a pirouette again, this time with the gun on full automatic. She couldn't very well aim with the gun poking out of her back. Spent casings arced past her face.

Another attacker fell, cut down by the indiscriminate bullets.

A fourth invader aimed carefully, putting a bullet through Olcha2's neck. Her head toppled backward, but her controls remained intact. Though her skull was attached only by a thin strip of skin and a bundle of cords, Olcha2 rotated her arms, walking backwards toward her attacker. The man looked as though he was going to vomit. But, keeping his concentration, he fired into her back, missing her head. The bullets again passed harmlessly though her gelatinous torso.

Olcha2 put her tentacled hands into the man's chest, turning off his biological heart in the same way a human might hit an off-switch on a malfunctioning computer.

While she was attached to the dying man's chest, yet another member of the assault team pulled a machete. He hacked at her arms and at her exposed breasts, severing a limb. Olcha2 kicked forward, rotating her hips into the strike. Her ceramic shinbone connected with his temple. The man's head cracked like an egg.

The final two attackers emptied their guns on Olcha2 and their already dead companions, turning her body into something resembling chicken wire. The pleasure of the assault overwhelmed Olcha2's circuits. She moaned once more as the automaton's brain overloaded.

From her vantage high on the roof, Olcha1 received the final signal and sighed.

Chapter 13

The outside of Club Olympus bristled with muscular statues bulging under the weight of a Parthenon-styled roof. Colored lights changing from red to blue to green illuminated the building. The chiseled frieze that ran the length of the roof featured bacchanalians scenes of nymphs and fawns performing craven acts.

Danny and his team, if you could call it that, watched from a roof across the street.

Danny thought it strange that the club wasn't surrounded by a line of wannabes waiting to get in. The front door was wide open. Yet only the occasional couple entered. No one exited, despite the late hour.

"So we just walk in?" said Danny.

"Yean, man, if you want to eat a fist." Jeremy loomed over Danny's shoulder. His buzz had worn off, making his speech clearer. "There's no line because there's no point. If you aren't on the list, you're not getting in."

Danny looked back at his crew which now consisted of the original member, Miles Birch, master of mathematics and amateur prognosticator; Ye-Rin, the prodigal spy; and Jeremy Hearse, noted biomechanic and a freakishly tall "dude."

Danny had to ask, even if the answer was obvious. "Is anyone here on the list?"

Miles didn't even look as though he'd acknowledged Danny's question. The man's social graces had degenerated even further as the evening wore on. Ye-Rin shook her head. Jeremy shrugged his gargantuan shoulders.

"Olcha, Mal, what do you think? Can you manufacture an invitation?"

Jeremy interrupted. "The security system is biological. Nothing that could be hacked so easily. They're going to want DNA, dude."

Olcha chirped back. "The file on Kang that Hardis gave me says that he was a member of Club Olympus."

"Super," said Danny. "So all we need to do is go back to Jeremy's shop, which is crawling with Party agents—"

"The other me killed quite a few of them," said Olcha.

"Yes, well done, Olcha. But, again, we'd have to go back over the roofs, break into Jeremy's office—"

"You didn't cut off his thumb?" said Ye-Rin with a shudder. "You used to be all about the thumbs."

"I only do that for identification," said Danny, all too aware of how some of the others were looking at him, as though he liked to wear necklaces made of human ears.

"I might be able to help," said Ye-Rin. "My boots are covered in his blood."

Danny shook his head, "So, what? We're going to wipe some blood on our hands and hope that fools the scanner?"

"Hey, don't harsh her plan. It could work." Jeremy had a long finger planted thoughtfully on his cheek again. "The entrance scanner is nothing like a fingerprint or blood test. The nano-bugs eat a bit of the member's sloughed off skin. Did you know how many skin cells we lose every minute?"

Danny quickly followed up on the thought before Miles could work out the math. "So if we just put Ye-Rin's shoe up to the monitor—"

"Forty one thousand, six hundred and sixty six point six to the hundredth decimal point," Miles interrupted.

Danny glared at him, but Miles remained unperturbed. Danny said, "This can't work. It will read her cells too."

Jeremy raised and lowered his eyebrows, "It will look like Kang's bringing guests, so there should be a bit of us floating around. Of course," Jeremy glanced around the group, "that also means they will know who's coming in the door."

Hardis had promised to run interference for them, feeding false positives and other glitches into the system. Entering Club Olympus using their DNA would paint a bright target on their location. Anybody hunting them, including the Party and the Russians, if Boris had survived the casino firefight, which there was a good chance that he did, would head for the club. If their enemies couldn't beat club security, they'd be waiting for them outside.

That being said, if they got the weapon, maybe Hardis would come through with an escort or maybe Danny could rig a dead-man switch to the weapon and bluff his way out of the club by threatening to blow up the entire city block.

Only one thing was certain. They weren't getting anywhere nearer Lee Kang-Sok's mystery weapon without walking into Club Olympus.

"Okay, then," said Danny. "What do we have to lose?"

"A few teeth if the security doesn't buy the ruse," said Jeremy.

The assessment was none too helpful. Once this mission was over, Danny would be none too sad to see the backs of Misters Hearse and Birch.

* * *

The lighting was negligible, and the music inside the club was the kind of thumping house beat admired by at least one of Danny's former neighbors. The cascade of sound was repetitive even in its changes, allowing dancers to get into a groove or for the other club-goers to ignore it and focus on the flow of conversation.

"I can't believe it was that easy," Danny shouted into Ye-Rin's ear.

"What?"

"I said, I can't believe—"

"Say it to Mal." Ye-Rin pointed toward her ear. "I can't hear you."

Danny took a breath, trying not to get frustrated. The club was loud, even though it was hardly crowded. The dance floor held a few couples and the predictable gyrations of a lone female ingénue out to demonstrate how at-one she was with the music. Her date didn't try to join her. That would have been disastrous for him. He leaned against a Grecian column looking bored. His eyes would inevitably wander to one of the other dancers, at which point the ingénue would move closer just to get his attention. While the outside had been difficult to navigate, Danny knew the inside of Club Olympus as well as he knew any ubiquitous club on the face of planet.

"Kang? You look different somehow."

A white guy with a frizzy blonde flat top and a 1980s fade haircut stood in front of Danny. The man's smile was much too wide for his face which could only charitably be described as horsy. These faults were overshadowed by the purple velvet jumpsuit trimmed in black.

Danny gave the fashion-challenged interloper an icy stare.

"Hey, now that's better. You almost look like Kang now," said the man. "The name's Mfume Will. This is my club. You're Danny Kim, right?"

Danny raised an eyebrow quizzically. This Eurotrash-looking club rat was supposed to be the greatest biomechanic alive? The subversive sponsor of nano-terrorism?

"I know what you're thinking," said Mfume. "It's the name right? You're thinking I should look more black. Damn, that's racist."

Mfume Will smiled even wider.

Danny shrugged by way of confirmation.

The simple gesture made the young man happy. He must use that joke often, thought Danny. No reason to spoil it.

"Let's move to a quieter location," said Mfume. "Bring your friends."

They walked past one of the club's many bars. Danny had to fight the urge to order a drink, a Johnny Walker Blue with two cubes of ice. After the breakup with Ye-Rin he'd gotten used to having a drink or three at night.

"That was a pretty clever trick you pulled on the door scanner," Mfume said over his shoulder as they walked. "It might have worked too. But you know what they say, forewarned is forearmed."

"You heard I was coming?"

Mfume waved away the question. Danny was left wondering how the man had known to expect them, when Danny himself hadn't known they would be coming to Club Olympus. Somebody must be keeping tabs on their whereabouts, but Hardis was supposed to be laying down smoke. Unless...

Danny ran an experiment.

"Hardis speaks very highly of your work."

Mfume led them into a private room separated from the club by only the sheerest of curtains. Yet as soon as the party was seated on the circular sofa and the curtain closed, the music of the club diminished.

"He should," said Mfume.

Danny's suspicions were confirmed. Hardis himself must have given Mfume the head's up. But it made no sense.

"It's some of my work," said Mfume, indicating the curtains. "Grown specifically to absorb and deflect noise."

"Dude!" said Jeremy. He put a hand to the curtain, running it up and down. "It looks like fabric, but I can feel its aura. It's a single, living organism."

"You have sensitive hands, my friend," said Mfume. "You must be Jeremy Hearse?"

"Yeah," Jeremy beamed. "I'm a big fan of your work. I can't tell you what an honor it is to meet you. I'm not worthy!" Jeremy made a little bowing motion.

Mfume acknowledged the obeisance with a nod. "I've seen some of your work. Not bad."

"This curtain is so macro," Jeremy continued, not realizing that Mfume had finished with him and that he was now to be no more regarded than a giant lamp.

A patronizing smile crossed Mfume's lips. Danny recognized it as the look of a self-certified genius condescending to speak to one of the hoi-polloi. "I seek a return to organic technology, removing humanity from the curse of right angles and steel."

Ye-Rin chipped in, "You want to go back to the Garden of Eden?"

Mfume's eyes lit up.

Danny knew how difficult it was not to brag in front of a woman like Ye-Rin, especially when she seemed receptive to the message of one's own greatness.

"Exactly," said Mfume, leaning forward till his elbows were on his knees. He gesticulated, talking with his hands at Ye-Rin. "Humanity is so messed up because our technology developed exactly opposite to our state of nature. We chose machines and pollution, killing nature instead of working with it."

"That's fiction," said Danny, playing bad cop to Ye-Rin's good cop.

"Fiction," said Mfume, turning red, which was quite a show for someone so white and might have been missed on anyone else in such a dark club were it not for his nearly albino skin, "is what's happening outside of us, here in Pyongyang. All these rockets blasting off into space and for what? What are they taking with them? Seeds of a new Earth? No!" Mfume banged on the table. "They're taking circuits and motherboards and electricity and steel and wires."

"You want them to blast off in a tree?" said Danny.

"I don't want them blasting off anywhere till they've gotten the picture that they can't rape Mother Nature and then fly off in search of another planet."

"Yet you are building weapons," said Ye-Rin.

"Yeah, of course, the Promeo Project was developed to take out the damn rockets."

Mentally, Danny dropped a half-dozen curse words. He didn't say any of them out loud, as he didn't want to endure Ye-Rin's holier-than-thou stare or to give away the fact that they did not, in fact, already know that the plan was to take out the rockets, the very lifeblood of the economy of Pyongyang and the central focus of every great power on the planet.

Danny thought of what Kang had said about Hardis and the Americans, about how they sought to reclaim military superiority.

If they had a weapon that could take down other rockets while leaving their own intact, they would reclaim their lead in the space race. If they went one step further, they could militarize space—though there were treaties to prevent it—but those treaties had not been ratified by North Korea. In fact, as far as Danny knew from his top secret clearance, every major had weapons in orbit.

But would the corporations allow an American coup?

Of course, the company that worked with the Americans would stand to profit exponentially from the failure of all the other companies. If this kind of thing were about to go down, Danny had been doing a poor job as head of security for his company, Next Wave.

Unless that was the company Hardis was using, which would be a perfect reason to force Danny to come work for him. And it also would explain why General Park Gee-Man, the spymaster for the Communist Party had been sniffing around Danny's apartment in the first place, hoping to recruit him.

If there was one thing Danny hated, besides elevators and airplanes and rockets, it was the feeling of losing control over his own life, over his own destiny. On a motorcycle, he was driving. With a gun, he was shooting.

It was beginning to look like Hardis had been playing Danny. Who else could Danny run to when his apartment got torched and when the Party apparatchiks started breathing heavy down his neck? Hardis might have even turned General Park onto Danny.

Hardis would have known that Danny couldn't turn to the weak-kneed bureaucrats in the Unified Korean government. By sending Boris to make a hit on Kang while Danny was present, Hardis had also made sure Danny wouldn't try to make an alliance with the Russians.

Danny's eye twitched, but he held his anger in check, replaying the last bit of the conversation so that he could chime in to the conversation naturally.

Mfume was off on another tangent on his environmentalist spiel. Jeremy was soaking it up. Ye-Rin looked calm, but Danny knew her too well. She wanted to jump up and scream "heretic" and burn poor Mfume at the stake. Miles was being his typical self. He had pulled out his dice and his book of hexagrams and was telling fortunes again, though whose, Danny couldn't say.

"Mfume," said Danny, "Hardis was worried that Kang still had access to materials from Promeo. We deleted Kang, but we can't be sure what he did or didn't have."

"That idiot?" said Mfume. "He has nothing. I don't know why Hardis insisted on working with him. Kang asked for a small sample to test the product. Stupid. I knew he had a lab set up on the other side of the river. He was trying to reverse engineer my process, as though these things grow on trees?"

"So, whatever he has is gone? And the Party can't make more?" Danny too wondered what it could have meant for Hardis to be working with Kang. Maybe he wanted to make the attack, when it happened, look like an act of aggression from the Party.

Meanwhile, Kang himself had been insistent that the weapon would free Korea from the capitalists. That would certainly be the case if rockets started blowing up willy-nilly.

Mfume was still ranting about Kang, "I knew from the copious amounts of Kang's DNA on the club scanner that he was no longer walking this world. But what a dumbass, right? Blowing up a plane and using Promeo to do it?"

"Right," said Danny, leading the man on, pumping him for information. "But Hardis doesn't know how he did that when it was supposed to take out rockets."

"Rockets-shmockets, planes-shmanes," said Mfume. "Like I told Hardis, as if he'd ever actually listen to anyone other than his reflection in a mirror, Promeo has a shelf life of a week before it begins to mutate. After that it doesn't just eat rocket fuel. It could eat any petroleum based products. Gasoline, butane, methane, a cigarette lighter for goodness's sake. Kang. What a dummy."

Danny could only nod. Yet, it hadn't been Kang, but General Park who had boarded the plane. Might the General have stolen the sample from Kang and hopped the plane in a bid to take the weapon out of the maniac's hands? He wouldn't have known about the weapon's propensity to change over time.

"Kang was no great intellect," said Danny. "His dying act was to lose a million Won to me at a Go-Stop table. Unfortunately, he departed this Earth before he could pay."

"What a tool." Mfume sneered, and his curled lip looked even more awkward than his smile.

"As you say," said Danny. "Nevertheless, Hardis is waiting on delivery of Promeo."

"Yeah, yeah. Hardis said to give you the package and that you'd deliver it to him tonight."

Mfume pulled a box from under the table. It was dark blue on top and bottom but had a light-blue, glowing ribbon around the middle.

"Despite the color, this is not a gift from Tiffany's," said Mfume, smiling at his own joke. "Don't open it. Tell Hardis that he has a week. After that, it mutates. A week later and it's dead. I bred in a kill switch. That way, if he needs more, he knows where to come."

"You're sure he can't make it himself," said Danny. "The Americans are technically advanced."

"Yeah, right," said Mfume, "which is why they're buying weapons from me now." He sat back on the couch, laying his arms out. It was his club and he was acting as if he owned the place, which was fine by Danny.

Mfume continued, "No. There's no way they can reproduce my work. It's all up here." He pointed toward his head. "Ask you friend there, Jeremy. He'll tell you that what we biomechanics do is unique."

Danny looked at Jeremy who was nodding and smiling at being included in such company as Mfume. That was all the confirmation Danny needed.

He struck Mfume squarely in the throat, collapsing his larynx. Once stuck together, the human larynx won't come apart absent medical intervention. Danny knew this. So did Ye-Rin. She rose to go, taking Miles and Jeremy, whose large mouth had dropped open, by the elbows.

Danny called out, "Help, can I get some help here? Mr. Will is choking? Is there a doctor?"

If Mfume Will had been using any emotio-ware to suss out violence before it happened, it wouldn't have been enough to catch Danny, simply because he hadn't decided to kill him till the moment Jeremy agreed that only Mfume could make the weapon. After that, Danny's reaction had been instantaneous. Certainly, security or the police would eventually review footage from that night and discover what had happened. But Danny's strike had come fast; and, just as fast, his hand fell on Mfume's shoulder pretending to assist the choking victim.

Guards entered the room. Ye-Rin and the two brains had already slipped out of the booth. Danny joined them.

"Olcha," he said, "trigger a fire alarm."

"The system is organic. There's not much for me to hack, Danny."

"Fine."

Danny pulled out his gun and fired several rounds into the ceiling. The guests panicked just as he hoped, heading for the exits. Danny, Ye-Rin, Jeremy, and Miles joined the throng of bodies heading out the door and, in the confusion of the moment, they slipped out of the club with the weapon, Promeo in hand.

*   *   *

Chaos reigned outside the club. The guest list streamed down the steps onto the sidewalk, where they formed into a shuffling, gawking mob.

Danny wondered why they hadn't fled farther, till he saw the black SUVs blocking egress from the club with weapons trained on the crowd.

"We want Danny Kim," a North Korean accent boomed over the crowd.

"Do you know who I am?" said a club-goer at the front who was dressed in an expensive suit and had an even more expensive hooker under each arm.

A rifle cracked, and the man dropped to the ground.

Apparently, they didn't care.

The rest of the high rollers decided to keep their mouths shut and file their grievances from behind their desks in the morning. More than a few had private security details that were now bodily blocking their clients.

Danny nodded at Ye-Rin. They mimicked the paid guards, posting themselves in front of Miles and Jeremy. Danny still had his gun drawn.

"You *stoopeed* bastards!" A voice shouted in a thick Russian accent from behind another SUV.

Danny recognized Boris and realized at once that the SUVs were not on the same team. In fact, now that he noticed it, Danny saw that as many guns were trained on each other as there were on the crowd. And not only Russians or Party members, a third group was in the middle of the mix, looking just as agitated.

"Comrades," the leader of the third group called out in broken English. It was a woman speaking in a harsh, Chinese accent. "We want Ye-Rin. You fight over Kim. We want the girl."

"*Pacheemoo*?" said Boris, "Why?"

"The bitch blew up my restaurant!"

Danny looked at Ye-Rin. She wrinkled her mouth—a sure sign of guilt.

"It was next to the YumYum, and I didn't do it, it was those Party thugs," she said. "Of course, they'd never have shot it up if I hadn't ridden my bike through it."

"Great," said Danny. "Olcha, any word from Hardis? Some air support would be appreciated."

Olcha took a second to respond. "He says it's the Chinese and the Russians and the Party. He can't get involved, says the air is lousy with drones. He says you'll just have to get creative."

Danny pulled his Doosan Bears baseball cap down even further over his forehead. If the drones in the sky spotted their smiling faces, they might take out the entire area. Miles tugged on Danny's sleeve.

"Not now, Miles."

"Um, Danny, the oracle says we can't take the weapon to Hardis."

Danny didn't take his eyes off the forces arrayed against them. "Did it say what we could do to survive?"

"Yes, it did actually, though I didn't understand it at the time," said Miles.

"And what's that?" said Danny.

"It said to give Ye-Rin to the noodle-lady."

Chapter 14

According to the biomechanic Mfume, whom he'd just killed in the private room of the club, prompting a mass evacuation of the premises, Danny held in his hands the most powerful weapon in the world, capable of taking down rockets and, with them, the world economy. And yet, he was powerless against a few dozen, highly trained operatives from three different countries armed with automatic weapons.

Olcha, his personal assistant program, spoke into Danny's ear. Normally a petulant Korean teenage girl who spoke in a Konglish accent, Olcha sounded as subdued as he could ever remember her being.

"Hardis identified the Chinese contingent," she said, "The woman is Choi Ree-Ree, or Sister Choi, as she is known—"

"I know who she is," said Danny. The woman was famous in spy circles for being a major player in the Chinese government in Pyongyang.

It was a well known secret that most embassy workers were also spies, which was one of the reasons the United States gave such a difficult civil service exam for its entrants. One had to be able to tell both how smart and how world savvy a potential spy recruit might be. Of course, the State Department also assumed that most potential employees taking the test had already been bought and paid for by opposing foreign governments. Point and counterpoint were all part of the delicate business of being a spy. You had to be able to play the long game or, when necessary, employ force strategically.

Ye-Rin stepped forward.

"Where are you going?" said Danny.

She turned to face him. She held no weapon in her hands and looked vulnerable in her plaid skirt. The tough biker jacket and boots only accentuated her fragile, teardrop face. Danny instinctively wanted to protect her and would have, even if he didn't still love her.

Ye-Rin spoke calmly. "Mal gave me the bad news too, Danny. That's Sister Choi out there."

"Along with Boris and some Party thugs. We can play them against each other."

"The Russians aren't stupid despite what you think," said Ye-Rin. "They won't move against Sister Choi. Miles is right. As long as she's here, things are going to get sorted out methodically and ruthlessly, which is no good for us."

"You're listening to Miles now?"

"He's been right all along."

"But you believe him?" Danny thought the whole world must be going crazy.

Ye-Rin looked at Miles with the sort of soft expression that she used to reserve for Danny. When her eyes returned to him, they were full of sorrow. "I believe in God," she said, "who works in stranger ways than these," she paused, "and I believe in you, Do-Song."

Standing on her tip-toes, she pecked Danny on the cheek before walking down the steps passing easily between groups of revelers that had drawn together either by the dictate of their security details or by instinct, like shivering animals huddled together.

When she reached the edge of the crowd and stepped forward, she called out. "I'm Ye-Rin." She continued walking forward.

"Good girl," said Sister Choi. "Boris, you idiot, don't you dare shoot that woman. And you other incompetents, where is Kang? The rest of you are morons. Hold your fire."

An escort of armed guards wearing black suits escorted Ye-Rin to the waiting vehicles that belonged to the Chinese delegation. Once she was inside, the Chinese drove away, pulling over the sidewalk to get past the Russians and the Party members who had flanked them on either side. There was a wide gap now in the middle and both sides were looking anxiously at each other and at the crowded stoop of the nightclub.

"Olcha," said Danny. "I've got an idea."

"What's that, sir?" Olcha sniffled.

The program sounded as if she'd been crying about losing Ye-Rin. He wished, not for the first time, that the programmers hadn't been so accurate in their work.

"I want you to paint the Russians with a targeting laser."

"But we aren't controlling any drones," said Olchaengi.

Danny smiled, "We know that, but they don't. More importantly they won't be able to tell who's painting them."

Olcha sounded happy again, "They'll think it's the Party!"

"Exactly," said Danny. "Stop talking and do it already."

Olcha's drone hovered a few feet over Danny's head. It would only take a few seconds to see if his plan worked. Meanwhile, Danny reached into his bag and switched on his home-made portable laser refractor, the one that had saved him and Miles when they emerged soaking wet from the river. If the Russians and North Koreans started blasting the bejeezus out of each other, he wanted to do everything in his power not to be collateral damage.

"Get ready to run," Danny said to Miles and Jeremy, not that he thought these two geeks had much experience at physical exertion, though Miles had swum the length of the Taedong river. It was amazing what a person could do with a gun to his head.

The Russian SUVs began moving erratically. With his trained eye, Danny could see they were taking evasive maneuvers.

One of the Party SUVs exploded, gutted with 50 caliber fire from an overhead drone. Of course, they had not been the ones painting the Russians, so the attack on their people seemed like an unprovoked act of aggression, one for which they quickly retaliated. The Party also started moving their vehicles and firing out of the windows.

Boris must have gotten the bright idea to mow down everyone in the crowd and sort out the bodies later. A red, targeting dot appeared in Danny's field of vision. There was an incoming missile. He could only hope that his DIY electronics assembly worked again.

Grabbing Miles and Jeremy, he ushered them down the steps away from the crowd that had started to flee in panic. Those with security details had been making an orderly retreat. They now grabbed their principals, those they'd sworn to protect, and ran, leaving behind screaming mistresses and the occasional boy-toy. They must have seen the exact same thing that Danny was seeing in his heads-up display. A countdown had begun, moving from ten to one.

The front of the club exploded. The missile hit one of the Grecian statues, taking out its chiseled abs. The statue collapsed and, with it, the section of the frieze it was holding. A woman screamed as she was crushed under the falling stone slab.

More warning lights flashed in Danny's field of vision. The ground around them erupted with small craters. The 50cals overhead had been unleashed. The bullets wouldn't be fooled by his electronic parlor trick.

Danny rushed underneath the fallen god, taking shelter beneath his outstretched arms. Ye-Rin would find this oddly poetic.

The thought of her with Sister Choi both pained and motivated him. Choi was not known for being merciful. But that also meant that she'd likely not kill Ye-Rin quickly. There would be time for a daring rescue, if they survived the present bloodbath.

Ye-Rin must have known as much, which is why she had put her faith in her god and in Danny Kim to act as that god's unwilling agent.

"Olcha, they're not using laser targeting anymore," he said. They must have drawn some conclusions from the way their missile went astray at the last second. "They've switched to putting bullets in anything that moves."

"Smoke?"

"Good thinking." Danny reached into his bag and withdrew a smoke grenade. It was amazing how such high-tech systems as the drones flying over them, as omnipotent and all seeing as the gods of old, could be fooled by something as primitive as smoke.

"When I pop smoke," said Danny to Miles and Jeremy, "We head to that entrance to the subway." Danny pointed to the corner of the street. "We have to get underground; get out of the kill zone. You won't be able to see through the smoke, so we have to hold hands."

The pair nodded. Danny released the smoke. He also grabbed another device, attaching it to Olchaengi's drone.

"Take it up about twenty meters in the other direction and release it," he told her.

"You said they were shooting anything that moves," Olcha pouted. "I move."

"Then move fast," said Danny.

Smoke filled the sidewalk. Danny ran, hauling the doughy Miles Birch in one hand and the giant Jeremy Hearse in the other. Danny couldn't see any better than they could, but he had good instincts and had been trained to operate, even in the smoke.

He heard the bullets impacting the ground around them. The Russian drones were firing into the smoke, no doubt using a non-random hunting pattern. If he bothered to ask Miles, the mathematician would likely tell them the probabilities of the Russians hitting them.

An SUV sped directly in front of them, it came out of nowhere in the fog and disappeared into smoke just as thick. The Russians were supplementing their hunting patterns with the grills of their armored cars. The Slavs could be ingenious when it came to killing.

Then the pounding stopped. Danny checked his display. Olcha had delivered her payload. It was a gimmick of his own design, a simple canister of confetti. It exploded, showering the street in burning ticker tape. The drones were shooting at the flaming paper targets.

"Olcha?"

"Ooh, pretty, Danny. Can you make me one? I want the ribbons to be pink and white."

"You are such a girl!"

"Humph, if you don't like it, you can always change my settings."

But Danny did like it and was glad to hear her responding. It meant that she hadn't been blown out of the air during the drone strike.

"Meet us in the arcade beneath the streets," said Danny. His feet found the steps leading down into the subway. The tunnels themselves extended deep below the city which was necessary since they'd served as bomb shelters in the decades before the invasion. Just below the city surface, however, the tunnels branched out in all directions, forming a pedestrian thoroughfare and a shopping arcade, which was also necessary given that the city might be covered in ice and snow half of the year. Much of the commercial life of Pyongyang, like its sister city Seoul, went on underground.

Once they reached these labyrinthine tunnels, Danny was sure he could lose the Russians and the Party goons. All he had to do then was to save Ye-Rin from the heavily armed Chinese and figure out how to save the world, without turning over one of the most advanced weapons systems ever created to a scheming American spy.

* * *

In a hidden corner of the underground shopping gallery, Danny and his two charges recovered their breath. Around them, the shops were covered by heavy steel shutters, closed for the night. The air was stale and shaded with the pale blue that weak florescent lights produce in the early morning hours. So many black market transactions happened in the tunnels that security cameras were destroyed almost as soon as they were placed. The tunnels were an electronic dead zone: perfect for hiding from the type of people searching for Danny Kim and his team.

"Just give me a second, okay, man?" Jeremy's fingers moved as he stared off into space.

Danny guessed that the biomechanic's optic enhancements were pouring data into his field of vision.

The detritus of a day's worth of shopping, receipts and empty paper cups, littered the floor waiting for the early morning cleaning crew to collect them. Old cigarette butts squirreled away in the corners were evidence of the crew's lackadaisical attitude toward their jobs. It was hard to watch somebody mess up your work over and over again and still care. Danny felt the same sort of frustration toward Miles and, to a lesser extent, Jeremy.

Since Miles had come into his life, Danny's cover had been blown, his apartment had been destroyed, and his girlfriend had been kidnapped. Well, Ye-Rin wasn't his girlfriend anymore, but she had been taken by the vicious Chinese spy they called Sister Choi.

Ye-Rin had gone of her own free will, to give Danny and the two-some a chance to escape. Yet he resented having to baby-sit the pair of them rather than mounting an immediate rescue.

"Okay, I'm in the backdoor of the system at my shop," said Jeremy. His fingers fluttered in the air. His eyes jumped back and forth as though he were watching a train pass. "Oh man, they took all my stuff. Assholes."

"What about Kang?"

"They didn't move him," Jeremy added triumphantly. "He's still connected. I'm going in now. Ugh."

A shiver ran down Jeremy's back. "I don't like to get so personal on a job like this. Kang was one ugly dude. I mean down deep in his soul."

"I don't need philosophy," said Danny. "Can you find out where his lab is hidden? The one that Mfume mentioned? We've got to figure out what's in this package before we hand it over."

Miles put down the book he was reading. The *I Ching* had finally begun to dry from its earlier wetting in the Taedong River. "You cannot hand it over to Hardis, Danny. The oracle says—"

"Again, no philosophy." Danny cut Miles off with a look. But a look was never enough with the nearly autistic man, so Danny put up a hand as well. "I'm an agent of the Unified Korean government. I'm not handing over this weapon to anyone, not even my own handlers, unless I believe that to be in the best interest of the people of this nation. But to find that out, I need information."

Jeremy clapped his hands together. His eyes focused again on Danny. "I got it. I got the location of the lab."

"Great," said Danny. "Send it to Olcha."

His personal program responded in a young, female voice only a second later. "I have it, Danny. Get this. It's not three blocks from your apartment."

"My ex-apartment," said Danny, again glaring a Miles who paid him no more heed than a fish might to a cloud in the sky.

"Olcha," said Danny. "I need you to split yourself again. Miles and Jeremy go with you in the drone. Get them to the lab safely. Don't let them do anything stupid, like stopping by your apartment, Miles, or paying for breakfast electronically." Danny reached into his bag. "Here's some cash. Walk a few blocks underground. Take a taxi. Speak as little as possible. You know the drill by now."

"Where are you going?" said Jeremy.

At least he was curious, thought Danny. Miles just stood there looking stupid.

"I'm going to save Ye-Rin." He handed Jeremy the case. "Don't even think of trying to steal this. The Americans are running interference for us. You won't survive a minute on the street if you betray us."

"Hey, man, I want to see what's in this case as bad as you. And since there's a corpse in my place of work, Kang's lab is sounding pretty good."

Danny nodded. "Miles. You go with Jeremy and Olcha, okay?" It occurred to Danny that he didn't actually care if the man stuck with them or if he wandered into traffic and got hit by a bus. Danny needed Jeremy's skill to interpret what Mfume had unleashed. Miles had become dead weight.

"As long as we're together in the end, Danny," said Miles. "The oracle says that we have to see this thing through together. That's what I was trying to tell you in your apartment."

Yes, in his apartment, his private little piece of forever, his getaway from the spirit-crushing existence of Pyongyang. Please bring that up again, thought Danny. It would make it easier to justify leaving the man behind the next time they came under heavy fire from the collective muscle of three national security forces.

"I'll collect Ye-Rin and meet you back at the lab," said Danny.

"And if you don't?" asked Jeremy.

"Have Miles ask the oracle what to do." If he didn't make it back to the lab, that would mean he was dead. At that point, it didn't much matter what happened. In two weeks, the weapon would be extinct. Danny had seen to it, by killing Mfume, that the Promeo Project could never be reproduced. But all of this, even the security of his country, was of secondary concern to Danny at that moment. His thoughts were entirely of Ye-Rin and of the torture Sister Choi might, even then, be inflicting upon her.

The drone led Miles and Jeremy in through the underground tunnels. Danny walked the other way.

"Olcha, open a link to Hardis."

Danny began to jog.

The gruff voice of the American General came through. "Oh, Danny boy, you're having a busy night. I'm surprised you had time to call."

"I'm ten minutes away from the corner of Mao Zedong Boulevard and Third Street. I need some heavy hardware."

"That's funny," said Hardis. "Because I'm looking at the maps, and I don't see you."

"I'm a spy, remember?"

"What's the game, Danny? I need the package that you received tonight. You remember our deal right? You and your friends walk away from this scott free as long as you play ball."

"Yes, sir," said Danny. He gritted his teeth to get rid of the bad taste of sucking up. "You'll get your package as soon as I recover Ye-Rin."

"The girl?" Hardis sounded stupefied. "Once you give me the package, the girl will be irrelevant. Sister Choi won't harm a former United Korea operative for nothing."

"That's not the Sister Choi I know, sir."

"I am not prepared to go to war with China over a former spy that wasn't even my own."

Danny recognized that the time was right for a little truth telling. "It won't be you attacking the Chinese. It will be the actions of a rogue Korean spy. That's been your game all along, right? Why stop playing now? Or have the stakes gotten too high?"

There was silence on the other end of the connection. Finally, Hardis spoke. "I won't insult your intelligence by saying that I didn't put you in the line of fire hoping you might get involved. I needed someone with your particular skill set. Hell, son, I know you and trust you. We worked together."

"You're right, sir. But you work with a lot of people. I had a less than pleasant chat with Boris this evening. So you'll forgive me if I don't particularly trust you. Sorry to be so blunt, sir." Danny passed a series of stairs that led to the street marking one of the exits for the shopping gallery. He kept running. "I'm five minutes away from that street corner."

Hardis laughed. "Blunt. That's what I always liked about you, Kim. Your little gook buddy bastards never say what they think. But you're American. Born and raised in the old U.S. of A."

Danny mounted steps leading toward the street level taking three at a time. As he emerged, a series of flood lights hit him in the eyes. His glasses polarized instantly. He saw a swarm of operatives coming toward him.

"Down in those damn tunnels?" said Hardis. "I hope you didn't catch something."

"He's clean. No package," reported one of the security operatives. They backed off a few paces. The lights were still in his eyes. He had no doubt that twenty different guns were pointed at his chest.

Hardis was nowhere to be seen. He spoke to Danny through the connection with Olchaengi. "Like I said, son. You're as American as me. So, I'm going to cut you some slack. Do what you gotta do. But remember the bigger picture."

Danny nodded. He was sure the General was watching him now and would see the gesture. "Sir, I need the location of the Chinese convoy. If they reach the consulate before I get to them, this becomes a suicide mission, and you know what that means regarding your chances of retrieving the package from wherever I've hidden it."

"They just crossed the river moving into the Chinese section of the city, heading deep into Commieville. They are on Martin Luther King Junior Avenue right now."

"Then I don't have a minute to lose."

"Which is why we've pulled out all the stops for you, Danny boy," said Hardis.

Danny could tell the man was beaming behind the microphone.

"Look at all you could have if you were working for the A team."

The spotlights cut out. Danny could make out the heavily armed operatives lining the street corner, blocking it with their vehicles and bodies. Five of them peeled away giving Danny a peek at what lay behind their impromptu barricade.

"Holy hell, sir."

"I know just how you feel, son." said Hardis, "Take care of your problems. We'll settle accounts afterward."

In the center of street stood a sleek, single-pilot drone. The smooth black chassis gave way to a pair of short wings equipped with jet propulsion engines currently oriented toward the ground for lift off. Danny eyed the harness rig underneath. He rolled under the rear tires, placing his back against the underbelly of the drone.

Immediately a chest rack closed over his torso while a seat popped under his backside, reminding him of a roller-coaster ride.

"You do know how to use one of these things, right?" Hardis spoke into his ear.

"Affirmative, sir. But while this is bad-ass. I can't attack from the air. This is an extraction, not a ground and pound."

"You'll find everything you need in the storage compartment located over the top of your right hip," said Hardis. "We didn't know exactly what you'd like, so we threw in the kitchen sink."

"Thank you, sir."

"Happy hunting, son."

"Olcha," said Danny, "are you plugged into this thing?"

"Affirmative, sir," she said in a voice that mocked his earlier awed response to Hardis. She was making fun of him.

"Olcha, tell me what I'm thinking right now."

"Sir, that is not pleasant, and without the body of the pleasure automaton, I don't think it's even possible, for me to—"

"Okay, then stop being a smart ass and take us up."

"Yes, sir," said Olcha. "Up we go."

The wash from the drone's twin jet engines stirred the dirt on the pavement blowing it toward the guards lining the street who covered their faces with their hands. Danny rose over the darkened streets of Pyongyang. In the distance, he could see the neon light of Reunification Square and, on the far side of the city, the lights across the Taedong River. His mind prompted Olcha in that direction and, as quick as thought, the drone responded, hurtling them into the night.

Chapter 15

The interior of the SUV was occluded by cigarette smoke. Ye-Rin tried to breathe shallowly. She fought the urge to crack a window. They wouldn't allow it. That would defeat the point of traveling in a heavily armored vehicle.

Ye-Rin sat on a leather bench seat facing the rear of the vehicle as it traveled through the now-empty streets of Pyongyang. The late nigh revelers were heading to bed. Meanwhile, the early morning crews had yet to finish their first cup of tea before leaving the house.

So far, they had traveled in silence. Mal informed Ye-Rin through the display in her glasses that they had been on the road for nearly twenty minutes. Long enough for them to be in just about any part of the city. At this time of night, traffic would not be an issue.

Finally, the source of the smoke leaned forward, her face coming through the mist like the figurehead on the front of a ship in a fog bank, just as worn and weathered as those wooden statues. The smoke had put a yellow patina on the woman's teeth. The first two fingers of her left hand looked as though she'd received a skin graft from an elephant. Her thin neck popped out of a tan pantsuit; her skull was topped with a sprawl of white hair, reminding Ye-Rin of a dandelion gone to seed.

"You're a hard person to track down," said Sister Choi. Her voice was so far past gravelly that it had become like a well-rutted, country road.

"It has been a busy week, *Unnie*."

"*Unnie*? Big sister is it?" The woman exhaled a column of smoke, though it made little aggregate impact on the amount of pollutant already in the vehicle's cabin. Ye-Rin wondered that the woman even bothered to take a drag on the slim cigarette. One could get nicotine poisoning just breathing in the air inside the SUV. "You know who I am then?"

"You are Sister Choi of the Chinese Consulate."

"Then you know I am not a woman to be trifled with?"

Ye-Rin nodded. Anyone could see that Sister Choi was a serious woman. She wore no adornment that would mark her as the bourgeois enemy of Chairman Mao's revolution. The starched tan pantsuit hardly revealed her femininity at all and was perhaps a blessing to the sagging physique of an older woman. Sister Choi's only vice could be found in the bluish color of her mop of hair—a color of hair dye unavailable to Western women due to a complete lack of demand. Even in her vanity, the woman maintained an imperturbable austerity. No one would pay money for that color. How very Communist.

"You blew up my restaurant today while I was having dinner with the Prime Minister of Pakistan." Sister Choi clucked her tongue. "Very inconvenient."

"I merely rode a scooter through the back door and out the front, *Unnie*. That cannot have caused much damage." Ye-Rin sat erect, emitting an aura of demureness out of every pore. It was a pose that every Korean woman practiced, yet so few could attain. Ye-Rin knew that her performance was flawless. In these moments she was the quintessential Korean woman. She was Ungyoe, the woman capable of restraining her bear-like passions to give birth to the man-god Tan-Gun, primogenitor of the Korean people.

"Oh, you're good." Sister Choi gave a little laugh that ended in a phlegmatic cough. "No, you did not cause the damage yourself. But you knew you were being followed."

"The people who disturbed you were present tonight. You could have had your vengeance."

"True." Sister Choi flicked the ashes of the cigarette into an ashtray built into the handle of the SUV. Ye-Rin had never seen one used for its actual purpose.

"But they were just low-level nobodies," said Sister Choi. "Not worth the cost of a bullet. Where was Park Gee-Man? Where was Lee Kang-Sok?"

Sister Choi looked off into the distance, as though she could see through the smoke or through the SUV's tinted, bullet-resistant glass.

Ah, thought Ye-Rin. So, picking her up outside the club was a pretense. Sister Choi wanted to interrogate her about the night's events, and the incident at the restaurant provided a suitable cover.

Ye-Rin knew she must speak carefully, "*Unnie*, I am sorry to tell you that Park Gee-Man died earlier yesterday morning in an unfortunate accident aboard an airplane."

"Enough pretense, foolish girl!" Sister Choi lashed out verbally.

Ye-Rin admired the change-up. It was exactly the sort of thing an expert interrogator should do to keep a prisoner off guard. Except that Ye-Rin had been trained by United Korea's top security agency, and Sister Choi must know this. Therefore, the mood swing might be real. Given Sister Choi's reputation, Ye-Rin was inclined to believe it.

"Forgive me, *Unnie*," Ye-Rin said in her most placating tone. "I should have understood that your question was rhetorical."

"You know perfectly well that it was not," said Sister Choi. "Now, tell me. What have you done with that no good *gaesaekki* Lee Kang-Sok?"

"He too is dead, *Unnie*." Ye-Rin saw no reason to lie to Sister Choi. She would need to budget her lies carefully if any were to be believed.

The wizened Chinese woman drew breath in through her teeth. She clicked her tongue against the roof of her mouth.

"That is too bad. He was—efficient," said Sister Choi. "But I wonder. Why did you take his body from the casino?"

Ye-Rin hung her head as though she had been caught out. If the woman's information network was so vast, she wondered that Sister Choi had to ask her any questions at all. Of course, the woman was a master spy. The demonstration of her knowledge was part of a performance, so that Ye-Rin would hesitate to lie about the most critical piece of information, the thing that Sister Choi did not know and had arranged this interview to learn about.

"*Unnie*, I carried him away because he owed my friend a sizable fortune. We thought to retrieve it even after his death."

"By taking him to the biomechanic Hearse?"

"As you say, *Unnie*. We thought that the biomechanic might be able to read Kang's program even after his death."

"I have heard of such a thing," said Sister Choi. "Did you succeed?"

"It was a delicate process," said Ye-Rin. "We found that the Party had wired his program to broadcast continually even after his death. They found us almost instantly."

"Of course they were watching him always. The honest have nothing to hide." Sister Choi said the words with confidence, but a slight tensing at the corners of her eyes led Ye-Rin to guess that the woman had not considered just how far the Party's information gathering methods would go. Let her think how her own precious Chinese regime was listening to Sister Choi's every word, her every bowel movement. Ye-Rin did not need Miles's skill at prognostication to know that Sister Choi would be paying a visit to a black market biomechanic within the week to have her own systems blocked against such intrusions. Too bad the best biomechanic on the market was dead and the other was on the run with Danny Kim.

Sister Choi continued. "This does not explain how you came to be at Club Olympus."

Ye-Rin spent one of her lies. "Hearse thought that another biomechanic named Mfume Will might be able to explain Kang's data."

"Ah. What did Mister Will have to say?"

"Unfortunately, Mister Will choked to death, *Unnie*."

Sister Choi extinguished her cigarette butt. She fixed Ye-Rin with a watery stare. "Did Mister Will give you anything, tell you anything? Anything about a weapon?"

There it was, thought Ye-Rin. Sister Choi was probing her about the Promeo Project. Of course. If the Chinese had gotten wind of the project, they would be peeing their collective pantsuits. They would do anything to secure the weapon. Ye-Rin decided to tell the truth, at least part of the truth.

"He bragged about his prowess with organic technology. He was saying that he had worked with Kang before, and then he began choking. None of his technology could save him from a tragic, though simple, death."

"This entire night was just a series of unfortunate circumstances, is that it?"

"I killed no one, Sister. I am a pacifist."

"Yet you leave a string of dead bodies wherever you go."

Ye-Rin sighed. "Those who are near me have been unlucky today."

Sister Choi emitted a coughing laugh. "You threaten me so prettily, child."

"I'm not sure what you mean, *Unnie*," said Ye-Rin. "If you have no more questions for me, may I go? I would like to attend the early morning prayer service at my church."

"From what you have told me, you may have much to confess, much good such superstition will do you," said Sister Choi. "But, no, you cannot leave just yet. There is still the matter of my ruined restaurant."

"I cannot pay that bill, *Unnie*," said Ye-Rin. "Will you make me do the dishes instead?"

Sister Choi chuckled and lit another slim cigarette. "Something like that, dear. Something like that. I do have a few more questions for you, but I think I need to convince you to answer them without evasion."

So, her lies had not been believed. Or Sister Choi suspected Ye-Rin was withholding information, which she was. Or maybe Sister Choi simply liked torturing people.

Mal screamed at Ye-Rin. Savage fonts flashed across her heads-up display. Mal was being hacked. His defenses were overcome in seconds.

"You see what we can do?" said Sister Choi. "But you do not grasp the implications perhaps."

"Mal?"

The program didn't respond.

Sister Choi lit another slim cigarette. "As you know, your personal program can read your mind almost. But did you know it is a two way street? It can sense your fear. It can also produce fear."

Instantly, Ye-Rin was terrified. The fear sprung up from her belly, traveling in goose bumps all the way to the tips of her fingers.

Sister Choi continued. "The mind is a powerful thing. What it believes, the whole body believes." She ashed her cigarette, regarding Ye-Rin coolly. "It's much less messy than the old methods of torture and more humane. For instance, in a situation such as yours, you might be afraid of being raped. But we no longer do that sort of thing."

There was no prelude. Nothing to warn Ye-Rin of what was about to happen.

Suddenly, she felt invisible hands sliding over her throat, pressing her down, choking her. She felt a man

enter her, felt with horror the unwelcome sensation
of penetration, bringing with it a visceral reaction of
pleasure and disgust.

Ye-Rin wanted to scream, but her throat, still
constricted, wouldn't respond.

Sister Choi snapped her fingers. The sensation
ceased. Ye-Rin could breathe. She threw up, spitting the
contents of her stomach onto the floorboard. Her whole
body shook.

"Come now dear, you used to do that sort of thing for
a living. You can't be as horrified as all that." Sister Choi
took a drag on her slim cigarette. "Water-boarding is so
twenty-first century. Who needs to fake drowning when
we can make you feel the real thing?"

Ye-Rin slipped down in her seat. She was underwater.
Her lungs couldn't stand it. She had to breathe. Only
there wasn't air. Great gulps of salty water raked the
back of her throat, burning as they entered her stomach
and lungs, filling up her chest. Ye-Rin clawed at her
throat and at the upholstery.

Again the sensation ceased.

"Now that you understand what we can do," said
Sister Choi calmly, "You see that, like you, I too am a
pacifist. I do not hurt people. I only want to have some
questions answered." She had come to the end of her
cigarette but didn't bother to dispose of the smoking
butt. Sister Choi stared into Ye-Rin's tear-filled eyes.
"Tell me what you know about the Prometheus Project."

Ye-Rin shook her head. Whatever they were doing, it
was all in her mind. They weren't actually hurting her,
though she supposed she might pass out if they made
her choke. But once unconscious, her body's natural
functions should reassert themselves.

"Suit yourself," said Sister Choi. "We're going to kill each of your family members in front of you." She held up a nicotine stained hand. "Not literally of course, but it will be all the same to your mind. It would be so much better if you had an optic implant, but we'll do our best. Please sit still." Sister Choi aimed a small revolver at Ye-Rin's chest and smiled.

In that moment, seconds away from a renewal of the torture, Ye-Rin felt the tires of the SUV crawling over the city pavement. She saw patterns in the swirling cigarette smoke. She noticed the silver flecks that decorated Choi's irises. It was amazing the way the mind could focus in moments of such high stress. Behind it all, Ye-Rin heard a buzzing sound that might have been a fly trapped in the ghoulish cloud bank of Sister Choi's smoke.

In the display inside Ye-Rin's glasses, her mother appeared. She looked happy. Suddenly a wooden baseball bat crushed the back of her mother's head. Ye-Rin shut her eyes, but she couldn't close her mind to the feeling of horror. Her brain was telling her that she'd just seen her mother brutally murdered.

* * *

From the top of a factory roof, high above the city, Danny watched the line of SUVs squeeze through the one-lane streets. Perhaps the city planners once intended the roads to be two-lane. Had the austere North Korean regime still been in place, the will of a city planner would have been law.

But with the rise of democracy had also come the sort of creeping capitalism so despised by every true Communist. On the open market, what supply was in more demand than the blind eye of a government official? Bribes were paid. Shops and homes were expanded; wooden hovels sprang up overnight, housing the families of economic migrants from Mongolia and northern China; till only these tiny alleys remained.

The modern roads of Kim Jung Un's Korean paradise had been invaded by the Mongol horde. Their hovels looked ancient. That was what the people remembered in their hearts and perhaps secretly wished to return to—a simpler way of life, a time before the corporations or the ghosts of super powers squabbled over their city, a time even before the Communists sealed the land behind a heavily-mined de-militarized zone.

The small streets below could have been in any pre-industrial Asian city, which had never been designed to accommodate cars. Were it not for the reinforced concrete instead of stone walls and were it not for the armored SUVs crawling along on bullet-proof tires rather than rickshaws drawn by the stout calves of sturdy men, these streets could have been out of an old painting.

Danny Kim intended to wreck that work of modern, urban art. Behind him, the black jets on the transport drone smoked in the cool night air. In his hands, Danny held new weapons of war born out of the industrialized, urban jungles. He had no tank, no artillery. The weapons he needed fit in the palm of his hand.

"Olcha, I want you to dive into the military drone they so thoughtfully provided," said Danny, tossing a piece of hardened plastic into the night sky. The new drone was similar to the one he used, in the same way a child's drawing was similar to a Picasso. The American drone was a quad-copter, equipped with four independent propellers that would allow the drone to do an aerial dance worthy of a Russian ballerina. He hoped that the part of Olcha stuck in the old drone, the one guiding

Miles and Jeremy to the not-so-secret lab of the former North Korean spy, didn't get jealous.

"I'm in." Olcha spoke directly into his ear by sending vibrations into his jaw that were translated into speech by the inner workings of god's own design.

"Oh, Danny, why can't you afford to buy me such a nice outfit?" said Olcha.

He could see the drone dancing on the breeze.

"I'll be sure to pick you up a Prada model if we survive this," said Danny.

"Arm the seekers, Olcha." Danny emptied his other hand over the side of the building. A swarm of small, beetle looking insects dropped toward the ground. Each bug was armed with a potent explosive.

It was this sort of asymmetric warfare that had altered the course of American military hegemony in the world. Any fool biomechanic could make these weapons.

Of course, the American tech was still the best. Without Hardis watching his back and cleaning his tracks electronically, the Chinese agents below would have seen the arrival of the transport drone and would have easily sensed the remote controlled explosive bugs that were, even now, barreling toward the exposed undersides of their expensively armored vehicles.

"Pick their weak spots, Olcha," said Danny. "We don't want to kill them if we don't have to. No sense pissing off any other major power tonight."

He had already shot up a bevy of Russian operatives at the casino and had killed the Party agents who'd breached his apartment. Spies made enemies. It was the nature of the business. But smart spies made enemies by choice, not by accident.

Olcha detonated the first explosive. The leading SUV bucked as its front tire ripped free from the axle. The heavy vehicle lurched, grinding to a halt in the narrow street. Doors slammed against concrete walls and wooden shanties as the guards tried to extricate themselves from the smoldering vehicle. The street was too tight. They couldn't get out.

The trailing SUV lit up almost simultaneously. The bugs had taken out the rear axle.

Danny didn't wait to see the result. He needed to be on the street, ready to extract Ye-Rin before the Chinese knew what hit them.

Hardis had identified Sister Choi's vehicle. Danny zeroed in on it.

"Olcha," he said, "I need to get down fast."

"Oh, Danny!" She sounded so excited.

"You guessed it. I'm switching to mannequin mode. Take me down and land soft, Olcha."

Danny relaxed his conscious mind. In mannequin mode, Olcha would pilot his body just as she had with the pleasure automaton. They had rehearsed the mode many times. It was perfect for a spy. A companion program could use mannequin mode to keep the body moving even if you passed out from pain or to keep swimming even when you were drowning. Or, like tonight, Olcha could turn his body into a trained Olympic gymnast, once she coupled his body to the sensors inside the drone.

Danny didn't like ceding control of his body to Olcha but could hardly catch a ride on her drone as he had off the apartment earlier. This descent required more speed, more finesse.

Olcha took over. She pumped subliminal, calming messages into his mind. He was totally at peace. In her electronic hands, Danny became a zen-master ninja.

* * *

Olcha, wearing Danny's body, stepped over the edge of the building and fell, catching a pipe, swinging into a somersault, bouncing lightly off a fire escape, grasping a power line, nearly tearing it free from its moorings.

Below her, a bug blew a circular hole in the roof of the target SUV.

Olcha rode the power cord like a zip line. Swinging down, she stuck a landing on top of the SUV, kneeling on one knee with Danny's gun drawn. Her drone scanned the street for any sign of attack. The Chinese agents in the SUVs behind the lead car were just now starting to open their doors. Olcha discouraged them with a series of exploding bugs that drove them back into the relative safety of their vehicles. Others she chased back in with a few well-placed rounds from Danny's gun.

Simultaneously, another bug dropped into the exposed SUV looking for Ye-Rin. The smoke inside the vehicle was much too thick to have come from the explosion that opened the vehicle's roof.

In the back of her mind, Olcha felt Danny begin to panic, fighting his way to the surface. He was fearful about what might have happened to Ye-Rin.

Olcha maintained control over his body. In her detached emotional state, she felt better able to manage whatever came next.

* * *

Ye-Rin heard the explosion. A small part of her knew that Danny had come to rescue her. But it had been so long since they'd parted. To Ye-Rin it felt like months. Sister Choi had seen to that, using Ye-Rin's own connection to Mal against her.

The crippling charge that took out the leading SUV barely registered in her consciousness. She'd been hearing explosions and gunshots for some time already as Sister Choi methodically went through Ye-Rin's family tree, ruthlessly slaying members of her family. Because all this was taking place in Ye-Rin's mind, Sister Choi was even able to murder family members who were long dead. Ye-Rin had seen her grandmother's body exhumed, yet in her sick, dream-like state, still alive. Ye-Rin watched as her beloved *halmoni* had been ripped apart by rabid dogs.

"Are you ready to talk now?" Sister Choi had asked afterwards. "If you are such a pacifist, how can you stand to watch those you love being killed?"

Ye-Rin had no answer. She knew that the images were not real. Yet she could not avoid seeing them. Sister Choi was giving her new, horrid memories, worse than a nightmare because they did not fade upon waking. She was already awake.

When the second SUV exploded, Ye-Rin's mind cleared a little. Sister Choi's attention must have wandered.

"Your boyfriend, I presume?" said the old woman, putting out a slim cigarette into a tray that held more stubs than a porcupine's back.

"What can he mean by this?" Sister Choi asked aloud. "He must know that we will kill you before he can ever get close enough."

Again, Ye-Rin had no answer. Her reason had nearly abandoned her, letting her animal instincts for self-preservation take over. She was blinking and breathing. Her heart was beating. She needed nothing else. Yet she forced her fragile mind to the surface, to regain control of her limbs that ached, not from exercise, but from the rigor of contracting them over and over again in horror.

Sister Choi lit another cigarette, then pointed a stub nosed revolver toward Ye-Rin's head. "I suppose I'm not so much of a pacifist as you after all. I hope you won't judge me too harshly." The old woman's nicotine-stained smile matched the color of her tan pantsuit.

"Nobody's perfect," whispered Ye-Rin.

"No, I suppose not," said the woman. Her finger tightened on the trigger.

Sister Choi had thought that Ye-Rin's barbed comment had been aimed at her. Nothing could be further from the truth.

Ye-Rin took the gun out of the woman's hand in one smooth motion. In surprise, Sister Choi's cigarette slipped out of her mouth, tumbling down the front of her uniform.

Ye-Rin put two bullets into Sister Choi's stomach. The smoke from the barrel mixed with the smoke already in the air. Sister Choi doubled over. Death would not come quickly. Ye-Rin's marksmanship had seen to that. She had renounced killing; yet Sister Choi would die. It was a new reality that Ye-Rin would have to deal with, one that she would have to seek forgiveness for, but at some other time. For now, she did not regret it.

The ceiling of the SUV exploded, letting in the night air. The smoky cabin emptied its lungs into the sky.

Ye-Rin felt a thump as a body hit the front of the roof.

Danny had come to rescue her from Sister Choi, but he had arrived too late to save Ye-Rin from herself.

* * *

The bottom of an aluminum security door crumpled under the heel of Danny's boot. He pushed it inward, careful not to disturb the breach alarm sensor located at the top of the doorframe. They crawled through. Unless the shabby building had motion sensors inside, which he doubted, the break-in wouldn't be discovered till someone showed up to work the next day. Of course, if Sister Choi's minions were still hunting them, they might notice the caved in hole in the bottom of the door. It was a risk he was willing to take. In such an industrialized area of the city, chances were slim that they would follow up on every broken window or bent door.

Inside the factory, machinery sat unused, heavy and silent in the dim red light of an exit sign. Ye-Rin slumped against one of the monolithic machines. Dust motes stirred where she disturbed the closed air.

Metal filings on the floor had been ground into splotches of motor oil by heavy work shoes. Danny guessed they were in some kind of facility dedicated to fabricating metal components for the rockets.

When Olcha had returned his body to his control, Danny had found himself dragging Ye-Rin through the cramped back alleys of the rougher side of Pyongyang.

Olcha might have been a gymnastic genius and a crack shot in his body, but she didn't have Danny's expertise in playing hide and seek. He knew that the first trick was to hide. While it was tempting to stay on the move, there were more chances of getting caught. When being pursued, unless your enemies had an experienced tracker, a simple storm drain or even an old cardboard box could be your best friend.

Danny didn't bother to ask Olcha to pull up a map. For the moment, it didn't matter where they were. They were temporarily safe from pursuit. And Danny needed to focus his attention on Ye-Rin.

Even if he didn't know her so intimately, Danny could tell that, clearly, something was not right.

Ye-Rin sat with her legs unceremoniously sprawled in front of her, staring at the palms of her upturned hands.

Through the bug that Olcha had sent into the cabin of the SUV, Danny had witnessed the scene in his heads-up display. While Olcha was controlling his body, pulling Ye-Rin out of the vehicle, tearing ruthlessly through the Chinese forces, Danny's mind had contemplated the image of Sister Choi's body, blood pouring from the torso, soaking her clothing, and of Ye-Rin holding the smoking gun.

Danny walked to the far side of the room on the pretext of securing their location.

"Mal," he asked. "What did they do to her?"

Mal responded in a monotone voice. If a machine could feel ashamed, thought Danny, this is what it might sound like, though he had no idea why Mal should beat himself up. Maybe the program blamed itself for not finding a way to keep its user out of danger.

"The Chinese hacked my program," said Mal. "They used my interface with Ye-Rin to show her terrible things. They made her feel things."

"Is that possible?"

Olcha didn't respond. Danny could sense her comforting and calming Mal in the same way Danny was caring for Ye-Rin. Danny would let her ask the questions. Being a fellow program, she could retrieve the whole story from him in a nanosecond.

"Oh, Danny," said Olcha. It was normal for her to pout like the school-girl that she was programmed to be. This time she sounded as though she were genuinely crying. "You know how I can sense your mood, reading your mind almost?"

"Sure."

"They—how can I explain? It's like they reversed the signal. Instead of reading fear, they created fear. They made her feel pain. They made her feel rape. They killed her family in her mind over and over again."

Anger flooded him, so palpable and raw that he was sure Olchaengi could read it like a neon billboard in Reunification Square. No wonder Ye-Rin had broken her vows and killed Sister Choi. The woman had gotten off lightly. Danny wouldn't have been so gentle.

"I'm analyzing the algorithm they used to take control of Mal," said Olcha. "Danny, it has American tech written all over it."

Was Hardis collaborating with the Chinese too? Danny didn't think so. Yet the man had hired a Russian hit squad to clean up his mess. And Hardis had manipulated Kang, using him as a middle-man between the Americans and the biomechanic Mfume Will.

Hardis must have used Kang so that he would have plausible deniability when the competitors' rockets started exploding in Pyongyang. Hardis could blame it on the disaffected North Koreans who wanted to drive the capitalist corporations out of their homeland.

General Park must have discovered Kang's plot and found it even too revolutionary for his notorious taste. For his interference, General Park died in what the press was describing as an airplane bombing but was, as Danny knew, caused by a mutated biomechanical weapon that had exploded on contact with the jet fuel.

No, it didn't make sense that Hardis was working with the Chinese. Yet Sister Choi had used American tech to torture Ye-Rin. Well, Sister Choi was a spy, thought Danny, maybe she'd stolen the algorithm.

"I'm going to kill Hardis," said Ye-Rin.

Danny had been concentrating on Olcha's analysis and on the problem at hand. He was surprised to hear Ye-Rin's voice and even more surprised to hear what she'd said. Hadn't she sworn off killing?

Some part of Danny was pleased to hear her threaten Hardis. Hadn't he wanted the ruthless Ye-Rin back? He'd dreamed of working together again. Wasn't that why he'd called her for help earlier that evening?

Yet, Danny couldn't suppress a shudder. It was what he'd wanted, but not like this. And, in a way, he was responsible. His call had put her in harm's way.

"Then you should kill me too," said Danny. He spoke honestly and on impulse. "If I hadn't brought you into this—"

"You weren't the one doing the digital rape."

He had nothing to say. So Danny kept silent. After several long minutes, Ye-Rin continued.

"Did we save the world?" The bitterness in her voice couldn't be mistaken.

"We're still working on that."

"Weren't we always working on that, Danny? Was there ever a time we weren't trying to save the world?"

"Somebody has to do it."

"That's what we were told," said Ye-Rin. "And you believed it. You didn't believe anything else, but you believed all that heroic bullshit."

The word sounded wrong coming from her lips. She was a Christian now. They didn't talk like that.

"Who are you to judge me?" said Ye-Rin.

"I'm not—"

"Don't lie to me. I can feel what you're feeling."

"How can you possibly—?" Danny looked at his drone. "Olcha?"

"Sorry, Danny," she said in a young girl's apologetic voice. Danny stared at the spot in the ceiling where Olcha's quad-copter hovered.

She continued, "I was checking out the American code. I might have accidentally opened a direct line between you and Ye-Rin. I can't feel emotion, so I couldn't sense the interface. I'll shut it off."

Danny had a thought. He needed Ye-Rin for what was to come later. And he cared about her. Maybe this was his chance to show her how much.

"Leave the connection open, Olcha."

"Cut it off," said Ye-Rin. "I don't want to know what you're feeling. And you definitely don't want to know what I'm feeling right now."

"You're wrong," said Danny. "Olcha, can you make it a two way street? Can we both feel what the other is feeling?"

"I can try."

Danny was angry, blind angry, the kind of angry where his eyes glassed over with red and he couldn't see anything until he'd put his fist through a sheet of drywall, which was unfortunate since, in Korea, every building was solid concrete. He hit a wall anyway. His knuckles hurt. His hand bled.

"You see what I'm like?" said Ye-Rin.

These emotions weren't his. Danny's mind could reason that much, though conscious thought was elusive. He pictured their first date, sailing down the Han river outside of Seoul after a hard day at the training course. It hadn't been a relaxing cruise, not in the traditional sense. They'd pushed the boat to its limit. The little rig hadn't broken. Neither had they. Not till Pyongyang.

We used to feel something, try to remember, Danny thought.

"You don't know what true love feels like," said Ye-Rin, looking up at him through red-rimmed eyes.

"Then show me."

"To be changed and to wait day after day for the other person to notice how healthy it was. For him to want that for you and for himself. But you never did. You wanted the killing, the thrill more than me."

"You want me to be a Christian?" said Danny. "Here's your chance. Show me what it feels like to believe."

The anger turned to pity. The feeling overwhelmed him, making his limbs feel heavy, like they'd filled with blood too thick to move. He wondered if any of his feelings were getting back to her through this flood. Danny realized that he might be unequally matched in this war of raw emotion.

"You know what it feels like to believe, Danny," said Ye-Rin. "You believe in yourself."

Who else is there? The thought was as automatic as breathing.

"There was me," Ye-Rin responded to him as though she were reading his mind, which she was. Of course, she'd always been able to read him much better than he could figure her out. This mind-meld probably wasn't doing much more than amplifying her normal ability.

"You could have believed me when I told you that there was a different way."

Danny wasn't speaking anymore. There didn't seem to be a need.

"Even if you don't believe in God, you could have believed in me. You could have believed that I believed."

Finally he put the words in his mouth, "I believed in you enough to call you for help."

Ye-Rin slapped her hands on her thighs. Her fingernails dug into skin. Danny felt the pain as if it was his own.

Ye-Rin spoke quietly, "You got what you wanted. I killed for you. I broke my promise to God. Are you happy?"

He wasn't. But Danny couldn't tell if that was his own feelings or if it had to do with the fact that Ye-Rin was so unbelievably miserable about killing Sister Choi.

"She tortured you. She raped you," said Danny.

"I could have turned the other cheek."

"And had her boot-mark on both sides of your face?"

"You just don't understand."

"What? I'm feeling everything you're feeling. What don't I understand?"

"How it feels to be separated from God. How it feels to be cut off from the source of life's meaning because of what I've done."

The next wave of emotion caught him off guard, like a rip tide, it pulled his feet out from under him, taking him deep into the ocean of Ye-Rin's despair. The sorrow she felt was not for the death of Sister Choi. That sense of mourning floated on the surface of a much stronger current. Ye-Rin felt cut off, adrift on that ocean. Her faith, that had become an anchor in her life, had been cast off. He could sense the words boiling up from inside, *why am I forsaken.*

Danny too felt the separation and alienation from this force that had been such a presence in Ye-Rin's life. His head ached. Danny's hands shook.

Then, all at once, another feeling traveled through the connection from Ye-Rin.

Peace surged through him.

The source of comfort did not arise from Ye-Rin's mind. Something else was speaking directly to her. Danny felt the presence of a third person enter into Ye-Rin's head and, through her, into his.

Part of Danny's mind moved toward that peace. He wanted it as he'd wanted nothing else in his life. He recognized that as the part of him that identified with Ye-Rin.

She drifted toward the peace. Danny started do follow the sense of her spirit, attuning to the peaceful companion.

A different part of Danny's mind rebelled, striking out violently at the source of calm. He didn't want to be controlled. He was in charge of his own fate. He did not ride elevators; Danny rode motorbikes. His mind screamed at the intruder.

"You're wrong," said Ye-Rin. "You only think you're in control. It's an illusion yet you believe it as though it were truth."

"Olcha, cut the connection." Danny nearly screamed the command. He panicked, needing desperately to be out of Ye-Rin's mind.

He felt himself go free. An atomic individual once more. Yet, part of the connection to Ye-Rin's emotions carried over. She'd given him her sense of peace like one might loan a book. And there was a new sensation as well. He felt alone. Truly alone. He missed their connection. Danny almost asked Olcha to reconnect them. He knew in his heart that Ye-Rin would agree.

But he also knew that she was not alone. That to connect to Ye-Rin meant connecting to the other; the one who was not Olcha or Mal. The one the very thought of whom filled him at once with fear and desire.

"What was that?" said Danny.

Olcha responded, "What was what, Danny?"

She couldn't feel emotions, thought Danny; so of course she hadn't sensed whatever it was that had come across Ye-Rin's connection.

"That was God," said Ye-Rin.

She looked up at him from the grungy floor of the machine shop. Her face was no longer contorted in a mask of shame and regret. If anything, she looked like one of the statues outside her church. The word "beatific" sprang to mind.

Danny didn't know what to believe.

"I missed God?" Olcha giggled. Her drone did a back flip. "*Chinja*? Really? I had so many questions. Like can he make me a real little girl like Pinocchio?"

"That's enough," said Danny.

"He said he forgave me," said Ye-Rin, "and that He can forgive you too, Danny."

Olcha interrupted in a pouty voice. "What about forgiving me? After all, the other me, the one with Hearse and Birch just killed two guards and hacked into Kang's secret lab. Maybe I need forgiving too."

Danny didn't follow up on Ye-Rin's offer. Danny had the bad luck to fall in with two of the only true believers in Pyongyang, Ye-Rin and Miles Birch.

"Olcha, give us some walking directions that don't take us by a bunch of angry Chinese?"

"Sure thing, Danny!" Olcha sounded as if she'd given him a bouncy salute.

He offered Ye-Rin a hand. "Are you ready to finish this?"

"Do I have to kill anyone else?" Ye-Rin rose to her feet.

"Would you?"

"I'd die first."

"As long as you don't die for me," said Danny.

"Someone already did that," she said, "And you didn't even say 'hello.'"

Chapter 16

At the lab, the biomechanic had ensconced himself in the middle of the fanciest looking equipment.

Danny didn't have a clue as to what the machines did. One seemed to have no purpose other than to emit an occasional, enthusiastic "ping!" Having guessed wrongly about the oscilloscope back at Jeremy's lab, Danny was in no hurry to further expose his ignorance.

The blue box containing the Promeo Project lay open on a table beside Jeremy.

Danny supposed he ought to be grateful that the lab hadn't already exploded, given their bad luck this evening. The unfortunate series of events had started with a simple knock at his door.

His unwelcome visitor and neighbor, Miles Birch, remained seated in the corner. He hadn't moved when Danny and Ye-Rin limped into the underground lab. Neither of the men had bothered to explain how the bodies of a pair of guards came to be lying at the bottom of the stairwell. Danny made a mental note to ask Olcha how the two science-types and an unarmed drone had accomplished that minor miracle.

Miles was engrossed, as usual, in his own private role-playing game. He rolled the dice and read the corresponding hexagram from the *I Ching*. Miles had become as obsessed with the dice as a player involved in a game of dungeons and dragons.

Danny crossed the white tiles of the lab, passing through a series of plastic sheets to get to Jeremy. His nose itched from the overwhelming smell of bleach.

Ye-Rin followed close behind.

Olcha, occupying the military drone and, at the same time, his own modest plastic model patrolled the skies outside the lab.

"What have you got so far?" Danny asked.

"Hey, man. Well, hello to you too!" Jeremy smiled, swiveling around in his chair. "Glad to see you alive and all that."

"Fine," said Danny. "How was your trip to the lab, Mr. Hearse? Were the travel accommodations to your liking?"

"It was cool, yeah," said Jeremy. "Olcha hacked the subway, got us our own personal train. We raided the dining car."

"A dining car. On a subway train?" said Ye-Rin, the incredulity dripping from her voice.

"Hey, I said she hacked the subway, not that we rode the subway," Jeremy replied. "She called in a full-size Pullman train complete with sleeping cars, though we didn't get a chance to rest much."

Danny spoke to Olcha, "Show off."

"What about the guards in the stairwell?" asked Ye-Rin.

Jeremy's smile faded a bit. "I don't remember. We got to this building and then I passed out. Guess I ate too fast or something."

Olcha whispered into Danny's ear, "Or I hacked his biomechanics. I turned him into a killing machine, Danny, using mannequin mode. He has some top of the line implants too. You should look into getting some upgrades. Did you know that he has two—?"

"Okay, forget it," Danny interrupted. What she had done was completely illegal and unethical. He'd have to have a talk with her programming about that. "What about the weapon?"

Jeremy stood up and motioned for them to follow him across the lab. Though the ceiling was three meters tall at least, Jeremy still walked with a hunch in his shoulders as though his head might hit the ceiling at any moment.

"Check this out." On the far side of the lab, they looked through a small window into a well-lit room that, for reasons known only to scientists, was filled with swarming bees.

"It's a blow up of the electron microscope," said Jeremy. "I wanted to show you what I'm seeing."

His long fingers tapped in the air using his biomechanical implants to manipulate the data on the wall-sized display.

"They're beautiful, man. Mfume Will was a genius."

"He will be missed," said Danny in a dry tone that Jeremy didn't seem to get.

"I can't wait to ask him about some of this stuff," Jeremy pointed at scrolling icons and jargon that

remained incomprehensible to Danny. He supposed
he could ask Olcha to translate it, but the biomechanic
would probably explain everything in his own, slow time.

Ye-Rin put a hand on Jeremy's elbow, "Mfume Will is
dead, Jeremy. You saw Danny kill him."

"Yeah, right," Jeremy rolled his eyes.

Danny suspected that Jeremy was into some pretty
heavy drugs, likely subsidized by his clandestine
biomechanics business. Maybe his brain had gotten fried
by some potent hallucinogen.

"Or maybe you should listen to me about what
Jeremy's got going on inside," Olcha whispered into his
ear. "If Mfume Will was wired like this guy, then—"

Danny answered both Jeremy and Olcha out loud.
"It doesn't matter how many lungs or hearts or spleens,
you only have one windpipe. No oxygen and it's bye-bye
brain time. If he lived, he'd be a vegetable."

"Only if didn't back himself up," said Jeremy.

Ye-Rin asked the question first. "Is that even
possible?"

Jeremy didn't respond right away. He continued
scrolling data across the screen, looking for something
specific. "For guys like us? No. For somebody like Mfume
Will? Maybe. Hell. I was this close." Jeremy squeezed
his fingers together. The display screen responded to the
gesture, zooming in on one of the motes buzzing around
the white room.

"That," said Jeremy, "is Mfume's gift to mankind."

"It looks like a mosquito mated with a firefly. I
thought he was into nanotech." said Danny.

"You're seeing that 'vampire firefly' at a nearly atomic
level. It's not a machine. It's completely bioengineered. It
is a walking, talking—well, not talking—robot as alive as

you and me." Jeremy pinched his fingers closer, zooming in on the bug's abdomen. "This little sucker literally eats rocket fuel. And when it does," Jeremy slapped his hands together, "Pop! The fuel interacts with a compound in its belly."

"But he's tiny," said Ye-Rin. "The explosion couldn't have taken out the airplane this morning."

"Yesterday morning." Jeremy reminded her that midnight had long ago come and gone. "Come on, Erin. Use your noggin for something other than snoggin. What happens if you smoke at a gas station?"

Danny followed up. "It only takes a spark."

"Bingo," said Jeremy. "These things breed like crazy. We're already into the fifth generation of the tiny sample I removed from the box. Now, imagine a million tiny sparks every time these things so much as sniff rocket fuel."

"Like lighting a match in a fireworks factory," said Danny.

Jeremy zoomed out and picked another cohort of bugs. "They mutate too, just like Mfume said." He tapped the glass window gently as if the bugs were in an aquarium display and might scatter at the sound of his touch. "A few of these girls are already shifting toward digesting fossil fuels."

"Brilliant," said Danny. "Hardis lets Promeo loose on the city, keeps his own rockets in their bays for a week, meanwhile the competition goes up in flames."

"Along with some airplanes and maybe a few car engines," added Jeremy. "I wouldn't want to be using a gas grill that next week."

Ye-Rin pensively pinched her lip. "They have a built-in kill switch, though? I mean, if they breed, why doesn't each succeeding generation get two weeks?"

Danny wished he'd thought of the question. The life spans might be short, but if they bred fast enough, like Jeremy said, then the little bugs would be as immortal as cockroaches.

"That's the genius of it." Jeremy pulled up several lines of code. "You see it's all in this section right here—"

Danny didn't need the science. Even if they gave the weapon to Hardis, and even if Hardis tried to use it, they could warn the other companies, minimizing the damage and maximizing the retaliation. There was only one thing Danny Kim needed to know.

"Bottom line. Can you reproduce Mfume Will's work?"

Jeremy looked at him as though he'd grown a third eye. "Could you bring an extinct species back to life?"

"I'm not a biomechanic," said Danny.

Jeremy sighed. A look of longing spread across his gargantuan forehead. "No, man. This is it. They're all dead in a matter of days. The mitochondria are passed along to each generation. They are all coded for extinction from the second the first one takes a breath."

Danny held up a hand, forestalling any further explanation. The next question was just as critical. "You said that they mutate. You can't reproduce the research, Will was confident about that, but could you selectively breed them?"

"To find a death resistant strain?" Jeremy's index finger scratched at the side of his face. "That's interesting, man, real interesting. In the wild, I'd say no, there's no way it could happen. But in a lab setting, with the right equipment—"

"I want you to get on that right away," said Danny.

"Danny, you couldn't possibly mean to—"

"Threaten the world's remaining super powers with a weapon to end all weapons?" said Danny. By his way of thinking, that was exactly what Kang had in mind when he gripped Danny's hand at the Go-Stop table. Kang had envisioned a Korean peninsula free from international intervention.

"Why not?" said Danny. "It's a game they've been playing for years."

He added to Jeremy, "Second, I need you to isolate those bugs that are already mutating, the ones that are already getting hungry for fossil fuels, gasoline, liquid petroleum gas—I need a batch of those."

Jeremy nodded his head. He obviously didn't understand what Danny had in mind, but there was no reason he should. Jeremy seemed content to play with the bizarre creatures of Mfume Will's invent. Danny was happy to accommodate Jeremy as long as he cooperated.

The set of Ye-Rin's jaw, however, indicated that she'd perfectly understood the nature of Danny's second request, or at least thought that she did. She was probably expecting him to sabotage any gas guzzling vehicles that threatened them. Danny had a much more specific target in mind.

However, there was one person whose approval Danny really needed before he could set his plan in motion.

* * *

"Will it work, Miles?"

"Let me ask the oracle."

"Damn it, Miles, I'm not asking for prognostication, I'm asking for a calculation. I need a mathematician, not a fortune teller."

Danny slammed his fist down on the table. Miles's black dice rattled on the surface, thankfully not enough to turn over and form a new hexagram, which Miles would have taken as a sign and insisted on doing a reading.

Danny had been awake too long. There hadn't been time to sleep since the Party agents knocked down the door to his apartment, looking to get at the dumpy mathematician sitting across from him. Now, having been in the lab several hours, the adrenaline of the chase had worn off. The bags under Danny's eyes felt like they held more rings than the inside of a Sequoia.

What Danny needed was a bit of Ye-Rin's patience and charm. But, with the nanotech research underway, Ye-Rin had asked Jeremy to take a look at the insidious American code that had been used by Sister Choi to hack her brain.

While the biomechanic had been mesmerized by the cleverness of the algorithm, he worked up a patch— which he'd first used on himself, the selfish bastard—and then ported to Mal and to Olcha for installation. Ye-Rin was rebooting, which was to say she was taking a nap while Mal poked around in her subconscious plugging the holes.

Danny would need to sleep too before the patch would take effect. Part of him didn't want to change. He yearned for the connection he'd felt to Ye-Rin earlier.

She'd once wanted the same thing, for them to be spiritually joined.

Danny could understand a biomechanical connection like the one they'd shared. But he couldn't wrap his head around a spiritual connection, especially without believing in a spirit in the first place.

In the same way, here he was, trying to explain a technical problem to Miles, who like Ye-Rin, was a true believer. Maybe that was the problem, thought Danny.

He tried a different approach.

"Okay, Miles," he said calmly. "Please ask the oracle the following question. It can handle specific questions, right?"

"Yes, of course. The more specific the better."

"Good. What I want to know is, given the rate of mutation, if each generation lived two weeks after birth, how quickly will the bugs spread across the planet?"

Ye-Rin spoke over his shoulder. She'd woken up. "He wants to know how soon food transports will start blowing up, Miles. He wants to know if, by releasing Mfume Will's nano-parasites, he'd unleash a worldwide famine by disrupting the international food supply."

Danny couldn't deny it. He didn't bother to try.

"Most nations rely on food imports, Danny," said Ye-Rin.

"That's why Korea grows enough rice to feed its own population. Food is a matter of national security. If other countries don't have the foresight—"

"You'd be putting a gun in the mouths of innocent children."

"I'm just asking the question."

"You're putting the fate of the world in the hands of a fortune teller?"

"Does your god have anything to add to the conversation?" said Danny.

"Take a nap, Danny," said Ye-Rin.

"I'm only going to use the weapon to bluff Hardis."

"You need to lie down before I put you down," Ye-Rin poked a forefinger into his chest.

"Strong words from a pacifist."

Miles looked up from his book. "The hexagram speaks of a global change. I think I was sent to give you this message."

"It's easy to see why you two were neighbors," said Ye-Rin, throwing her hands up into the air in defeat. "You're both delusional. One of you thinks he can make sense of the world with a gun and the other with numbers. You're mentally ill."

"Numbers do not lie," said Miles. Her criticism had bounced off of him like a hacky-sack off a brick wall. "The message is clear."

"Clearly from the devil, you mean," said Ye-Rin.

Danny didn't bother to point out that the person who believed in an actual devil was calling the two of them delusional.

At this point in his familiar rant against Ye-Rin's religion, an interesting thing happened. Danny's mind hit an unexpected road bump. If Ye-Rin was delusional, what had he experienced when they were sharing a connection in the factory?

"I hate to interrupt," said Jeremy. "Erin, you shouldn't get so worked up. It's a done deal. The bugs you asked for are ready, Danny. I can't reproduce Mfume Will's work, but I hacked it all right. Each generation will last two weeks from the time they're born, not from the time the original generation is released. It took some doing. Like I said, I couldn't reproduce his work if I wanted to, but I changed a small snippet of their mitochondrial code. If released, these buggers will reproduce perpetually."

Jeremy put three packages on the table. The first was the blue box, closed again, emitting a light-blue glow. Next to it was a smaller white box that had been labeled with a black magic marker: "Pandora." Apparently the big man had a sense of humor.

"Here's that other project you asked about." Jeremy placed a small rubber vial next to Danny. "There ain't many of them. Plus, this batch of mutant badness still has the original two week shelf-life. Don't open it anywhere around me, okay?"

"Not if I can help it," said Danny.

Danny gathered up the two packages, slipping them inside his jacket. The rubber tube he placed in his front pocket where it would be easily accessible.

"The lab is clean? No way to trace what we've been up to?" said Danny. "You know what they'll do to you if they find you with any of this stuff." Danny patted the packages.

"The lab's cleaner than bleach, man," said Jeremy. "You going to kill me now like you did Mfume?"

The tall biomechanic was smiling, but Danny could tell that his question came in earnest.

"No," said Danny. "Ye-Rin is too sweet on you."

Did he think that Jeremy had actually wiped all the data he'd gathered about the bugs? No. But Danny was fairly sure that the man had been honest about his inability to reverse engineer the tiny creatures. Let him keep the research. If he ever figured it out, that would be a problem for another spy. As of that moment, all of the vampire fireflies in existence were in Danny's hands as was the fate of the world.

Now, he thought, I can finally get some sleep.

Chapter 17

He awoke with a bang.

Danny's hand went to his gun.

Opening his eyes, he checked the display in his glasses—which he'd gone to sleep wearing, fearing just such an eventuality. A small video screen showed shock troops pouring into the building from the street. The breach of the lab's inner door must have been the source of the rude awakening. The smell of the explosion was just beginning to reach his nose.

Replacing the gun in its holster, Danny sat up on the rubber floor mat that had served as a makeshift bed. He got to his feet. From what he'd seen, there were too many to fight and too many to run from. He placed his hand instead on the rubber vial in his jacket pocket. He held the special treat that Jeremy Hearse had supplied in case push came to shove.

Danny wasn't surprised about being attacked. It was always a possibility that one of the groups would get lucky and find them. Maybe the Party had figured out where they were after two of their guards failed to check in.

The fact of the attack didn't bother him. What did bug him was that Olcha hadn't informed him about the small army that was laying siege to the building. Surely they couldn't have cordoned off the entire city block without her noticing.

He asked her as much, but she didn't respond. Danny checked on her status. The flimsy plastic drone was still high in the sky, sending him video of the enemy positions around the building. The view from the military quad-copter was coming from inside the lab itself. Danny saw the astonished faces of his makeshift team, Ye-Rin, Miles, and Jeremy.

As he slowly walked toward the group, emerging from the smoke of the breaching charge to join his compatriots, Danny saw himself reflected by the drone. And he saw at least ten high-powered rifles pointed at his chest.

The display on his glasses showed the time. 9:31 a.m. Less than ninety minutes from the time he'd lain down, not even a full REM cycle, though under sleep deprivation scenarios, he knew that people could go into REM much quicker. He didn't remember having dreamed. And he still felt like crap—which was bound to be the case REM or no REM.

"Danny Kim, time to rise and shine. We have a full day ahead of us."

The American accent unmistakably belonged to Sherman Tecumseh Hardis. The man himself, however, was nowhere to be seen. He must have accompanied the American team remotely.

Well, it figured that Hardis was behind the attack, thought Danny. Had it been any other team, they would have shot first and answered questions later.

"You weren't thinking about skipping town with my package were you?"

"I'd never dream of it, sir."

"That's good. Of course, just in case, we borrowed your companion program, Olchaengi, I think you call her? Cute gal. She and MacArthur have been having a blast together."

Danny felt blood rushing to his face. He forced himself to remain calm. She was just a computer program. With his training and, heck, just out of plain common sense, he knew better than to personify Olcha.

He couldn't help it. To him, Olcha was as much a member of the team as Ye-Rin and even more so than Miles or Jeremy.

"She's telling us you're plenty pissed. Don't fret. We'll give her back, right as rain. After all, we want you to come with us. We need you to cooperate, right? Else you'll unleash the holy hell that you've got in your pockets?"

Danny rolled the rubber vial around in the palm of his hand. He thought angry thoughts about vengeance. If Hardis was monitoring his emotions, Danny could use that in his favor during what had now become a negotiation for all their lives.

"Calm down, son. Don't do anything stupid. I just want to talk."

"Fine. Let's talk. Face to face."

"Of course, of course. One second. Let me give the order to my people."

The lead agent stood at attention in full body armor. He put a hand to his ear. It was a good bit of playacting. No one needed to cradle an earbud these days, not with the implants that channeled vibrations from your jawbone to your eardrum. The Americans always had such a sense of style about them. They were all about the shock and awe. The shock had come with them blowing through the door. The awe took showmanship.

The agent nodded his head.

Before Danny could move, the agent swiveled his rifle and put two rounds through the chest of Jeremy Hearse. The tall man fell like a demolitioned building, crumpling from the inside, his stomach hitting his knees as his body collapsed to the floor.

"Micro, man. Real micro," Jeremy wheezed a final complaint.

Ye-Rin, despite her training, or because she'd been so far removed from it lately, screamed and flung herself across the biomechanic as if to protect him.

The gesture, though sweet and heroic, was futile. They needn't spend any more rounds on the man. A double tap to the chest typically got followed up by a bullet to the head, but that was more in the way of a formality.

"The math geek is next followed by the girl," said the bodiless voice of General Hardis. "I needed to let you know how serious I am about getting the packages that you're carrying."

Danny pulled his eyes away from the blood pooling around Jeremy's back. He looked at the military quad-copter which was the source of Hardis's eyes, ears, and mouth.

"Crystal clear, sir."

"Good. You three, follow my people back to my place."

"No," said Danny.

The American agent automatically pointed his rifle at Miles with his finger on the trigger.

Danny needed to resist a little. He hated this sense of being out of control, of feeling that his fate was not in his own hands. But that wasn't the only reason he needed to stall. He couldn't give in too easily, not even in the face of an immediate threat to another member of his team. Hardis had taken out Jeremy. Danny had to make Hardis compromise on something. Otherwise, the negotiations would be as dead as he would eventually be.

"I'm not going anywhere till you give Olcha back and till I see a medic at my friend's side."

"You were in the war, Danny. You've seen that kind of wound before," said Hardis. "You know there's no hope."

"Olcha and a medic, General."

"Fine."

A young woman wearing a red patch over the right bicep of her body armor hurried forward. She knelt beside Jeremy. He knew that General Hardis might be right about the biomechanic's prognosis, but there were things that could be done to at least ease the pain.

"Olcha?"

"I'm here, Danny."

There was no telling of course whether she were really the Olcha that he knew and loved or whether she'd been fully compromised. Nothing short of a full diagnostic could tell him that. When they'd hacker her, they would have gotten access to every memory she ever had. It wasn't as though he could ask her a question that only the two of them knew. If she knew it, they knew it.

One thing he could do, though. "Olcha, disconnect from the drones. We're running silent from here on out."

He could disconnect from the system entirely. He could stop broadcasting. At least Hardis could no longer access his emotions, unless the Americans had found a way to compromise the biomechanical hardware inserted into his body. If so, he'd be broadcasting and never know it, just like poor Kang-Sok.

Danny couldn't deny that possibility. Normally, a foreign agent shouldn't have to worry about another country snooping via his hardware, but given how cozy the Unified Korean government had always been with the U.S., there was a chance that the Americans were able to listen in. Regardless, he didn't have to make it easy for them.

"Let's go." Danny nodded to the lead agent who turned, ushering the three of them out of the lab and into the gray morning light of Pyongyang.

*　*　*

"You've been busy, Danny."

They were back on the fourth floor, *sa cheung*, the floor of death in Korean, inside the gray walls of the concrete interrogation room where they'd originally met General Hardis. The trip to the inconspicuous office building in the heart of Pyongyang that housed the American spy operation had been uneventful. The placid façades of dusty communist buildings conveyed no reassurance.

Ye-Rin had quietly cried most of the way. Jeremy had been an asset and a friend. She blamed herself for losing one of their own. Danny didn't need to be connected with her to understand what she was thinking. She was walking through the what-might-have-beens. For instance, if she hadn't dragged Kang's body to Jeremy, he'd be knee deep in illegal optic implants today.

Danny knew the feeling. He felt the same about getting Ye-Rin involved in this business. He'd known somebody was after the mathematician and had asked Ye-Rin for help. He didn't know that somebody would include the three remaining superpowers and the Communist Party of the former North Korean government. He'd seen it as an excuse to see her again, to working together.

Inside the interrogation room, Danny and his team had ignored the proffered chairs—two chairs, same as last time, so that someone would automatically be the odd man out, a way of psychologically breaking up a team before bringing out the big guns like torture or bribes. Instead, they had collapsed onto the floor following Miles's example from the previous evening.

Hardis stood facing away from them with his arms folded behind the back of his khaki, uniform-looking clothes. It looked as though the man were trying to channel the spirit of General Patton. Maybe he would slap Danny across the face to complete the act, just as old blood and guts Patton had done to an enlisted man during the second World War.

Instead, Hardis merely continued his monologue, "Kang is dead. Boris is royally pissed. Sister Choi won't be eating dumplings anytime soon, if you know what I mean."

Ye-Rin looked up.

Hardis glanced over. "Oh, you didn't kill her. Gut shots are too slow for modern medicine."

Maybe Ye-Rin had subconsciously known that, thought Danny. But it would have had to have been a deeply subconscious act given how angry she'd felt when their minds had been connected.

Danny wondered if that was how Hardis intended to come at them, to torture them using the code the Chinese had copied from the Americans. If so, he was going to be disappointed. Danny and Ye-Rin had been patched. Miles didn't have an implant to begin with.

"Let's get down to brass tacks, Danny."

Hardis loved tossing around little idioms like that. He was speaking American to Danny Kim, a boy who'd grown up in the States.

"Cards on the table, son. What exactly did you have in mind with those boxes you got from those biochemical bastards?"

"I was going to use them for decoration, sir. Have you heard of feng shui?"

"Clever. But we heard the conversation you had with your buddies, of course. We've always been one step ahead of you, haven't we? Agent Birch? Care to tell us what Danny boy has planned?"

The General had to be joking, thought Danny. Their geeky companion sat beside them on the cold concrete floor. Was General Hardis seriously saying that the doughy, Miles Birch was an agent of the U.S. government?

Miles spoke up. "The oracle says that he is the bringer of change, the causer of the plague. He will open Pandora's box."

"Miles?" said Ye-Rin.

"Agent Miles Birch is one of our best and brightest, well, at what he does at any rate."

"And just what is that," said Danny, thinking he should have let the man take a bullet back at his apartment and saved himself a hell of a lot of trouble.

"He's a data analyst. A very quirky one. But he's the best at predicting the proverbial future."

"Miles, you son of a bitch," said Danny.

"Now, now," said Hardis. "Don't take it out on the man. Don't act like you've never counterspied. You were just too proud. You overlooked Mr. Miles."

"I'll recognize him next time I see him alone on the street," said Danny.

Miles turned white. He swallowed forcefully.

"You won't lift a finger toward him, Danny, and you want to know why?"

Danny did not want to know. So he didn't ask.

"Because the Russians, the Chinese, and the shadow government of North Korea want you dead after tonight." Hardis paused for effect. "Do you think the Unified Korean government is going to protect you? No. No, sir. You are ours, Danny Kim. You are once again property of the USA. You were born and bred American, son, and it's high time you started acting that way."

Hardis had used Danny to acquire the Promeo project in a way that couldn't be traced back to the Americans. Kang must have been Hardis's first choice, but the man proved entirely predictable in his betrayal. Even their Party's own top operative, General Park Gee-Man had suspected Kang. Therefore, Hardis needed someone else. Someone just like Danny Kim.

"You thought you made it into KATUSA back in the day on your own merit, son? I asked for you personally, did you know that?"

Danny had not known. He thought his selection for the coveted KATUSA liaison role had been based on his skill with English and level of comfort with the American troops.

"They stick *gyopos* like you as far out of the way as they possibly can," said Hardis. "They don't trust your loyalty. Besides, the Koreans don't put anybody in KATUSA that's not already on the road to becoming a spy. That's all KATUSA is, just a way of keeping tabs on us way-gook-een, us foreigners. Hell, son, after I asked for you I knew they'd eventually have to put you in the spy game. I knew I'd get my chance sooner or later. I'd bide my time till the time was right. And here you are. Come full circle." Hardis turned and faced Danny. He waved his hand through the air. "I know it must have been tough on you not knowing my purpose. But I always saw big things for you, Danny. I want you to come on board willingly, as my lieutenant, second only to me, in Pyongyang."

"And what if I say no?"

"Take your chances on the street. You and your friend, Ye-Rin. How long do you think she'll last?"

Not long, thought Danny, not with Sister Choi getting bullets dug out of her abdomen even as they spoke.

Hardis turned to the dumpy analyst. "Miles, you can go now. I know it's been a hard night on you, but you performed admirably. There'll be a medal in it for you."

"I have to stay," said Miles. "The oracle said Danny and I had to stay together for the mission to be complete. It is the only reason I agreed to this plan. The oracle said there was no other way."

In his most reassuring tone, Hardis said, "The mission is over now. We got the weapon. It's in American hands. It's all over."

Miles didn't move. Hardis, shrugging his shoulders, stopped trying to cajole him. Danny was amused to learn that the master spy had no more control over Miles than Danny did.

"Technically I've got the weapons," said Danny.

"We'd shoot you before you could open the boxes," said Hardis. "We designed the emotio-ware that the casinos use, you know."

Danny had rather suspected the Americans had something at least as advanced as the monitoring system at the casino in their interrogation suite.

"What do you plan to do with the weapon?" said Danny.

"Do you want me to monologue, like a super villain?" said Hardis. "You know what I'm going to do. I'm going to take that blue box and destroy our competition here in Pyongyang, everyone except for your employer Next Wave, and then I'm going to do exactly what you planned on doing. I'm going to blackmail the entire world with that white box in your pocket."

"You want worldwide American hegemony again," said Danny.

"Just like God intended."

Ye-Rin coughed. Apparently, she thought god had other things in mind.

If so, perhaps god shouldn't have put General Hardis in charge. The man appeared to have everything sewn up tight. With Ye-Rin's life on the line, he didn't dare oppose Hardis openly.

That left only one other option.

"I'll do it," said Danny. "I'll work for you."

He endured an incredulous stare from Ye-Rin, complete with both eyebrows arched at the same time.

"Kim Do-Song!" she said.

Olcha normally would have teased him about Ye-Rin using his full name. His companion program had been rather subdued since being returned to him.

"On a few conditions of course," said Danny. He took the white and the blue boxes out of the inner pockets of his jacket. "You triple my pay."

"Done," said Hardis. He was smiling widely now and had pulled two cigars out of his shirt pocket in anticipation of celebrating the deal.

"And the position becomes permanent, now, before I hand these over."

"Of course, I wouldn't have it any other way," said Hardis. Speaking into the air he added, "I told you he was smart, didn't I MacArthur?"

"You did, sir." Hardis's companion commented through the speakers in the ceiling which had probably been meant to blast heavy metal music at sleep deprived prisoners.

"Finally, you agree that Boris can go away. I'll do it myself. But he and I can't be in the same city. If he doesn't leave, I have permission to terminate him."

"Sure thing, Danny, can't wait to see how you do it. It's going to be fun working together again."

"Sir, I want to hear the confirmation."

"MacArthur? Do it. Everything he said. Read him the code."

"Done, sir. Order number 579801."

Hardis handed a cigar toward Danny, "There it is. Signed, sealed, and last but not least, delivered."

Danny handed the glowing blue packet to Hardis along with the white box marked Pandora.

Miles sat on the floor unperturbed. Ye-Rin stared at the floor, unable to look Danny in the eyes.

That was fine. She would understand in time, he thought. Turning over the packages to Hardis was how it had to happen. It was the only way Danny could protect her.

Hardis raised his lighter, ready to ignite Danny's cigar. The thick bundle of wrapped leaves had been imported from Cuba. It had taken a long voyage around the world. Such cigars could not be flown, not stored in a luggage compartment where they might freeze. They had to be treated with care, which was why only a dolt lit an expensive cigar with a cigarette lighter. The smell of the cheap fuel would lodge on your tongue as you brought the cigar to life with a few deep, flamatious breaths. Purists used matches. The elite smoker, like Hardis, used a clean-burning butane lighter.

He offered to light Danny's cigar first. Danny waved him away, pulling out a small box of matches that bore the label of Club Olympus.

Hardis shook his head disapprovingly as Danny lit the match and let the small flame grow to engulf the end of the fine cigar.

"What about the rubber tubey thing? You keeping that for yourself?" said Hardis. "Never mind. You're my lieutenant now. Do what you want."

He flipped open his lighter.

"I already did," said Danny.

Hardis's eyebrows shot up. "Oh, really?"

Danny cocked his head to one side, breathing out a deep cloud of cigar smoke. "I opened it before we entered this room."

"What?"

It happened almost in slow motion. Hardis's lighter sent a thin blue flame into the air as his thumb hit the ignition switch. The General's eyes widened at the sight of the flame. The cigar fell from his lips. Danny ducked his head under his arm. The butane lighter exploded in Hardis's hand, sending bits of metal shrapnel through his eyes and into his brainpan.

Ye-Rin and Miles shouted as they got pelted by flaming bits of molten metal. They stood up, dancing around at the sudden explosion and the sharp pain that followed.

Hardis lay on the concrete floor, his lifeblood escaping from his face and his neck; his damaged mind incapable of forming a sentence.

"I'm calling for medical aid, sir," said MacArthur.

"Belay that order, program," Danny ordered.

"What do you mean?" MacArthur's splutter sounded like a discombobulated yet still pompous servant. His programmers had done a good job.

"I mean that General Hardis is incapable of command decisions. Therefore, he is relieved of command and I, as his second in command, am in charge of this facility and of American operations in Pyongyang. Do you understand?"

"Yes."

"MacArthur, put the building on lock down. Tell everyone there's a natural gas leak and they are to exit the buildings. They are not to come into the office for two weeks, nor are they to operate any machinery that uses fossil fuels. Am I clear?"

"That will sound a bit strange, sir."

"It's a spy agency. Strange is normal. When things start exploding around the city, they'll figure it out."

Olcha now spoke up a little timidly, "Is Hardis dying, Danny? Is he in much pain?"

"I'm afraid so, Olcha, on both accounts."

"Good," she said simply. "Danny can I have permission to leave silent mode? There's something I'd like to do."

"Sure, Olcha," said Danny. He hoped that she really was his program after all, and that this wasn't some sort of trick. Yet he didn't see how his plan could be foiled now. He had gotten Jeremy to isolate those bugs knowing that they'd digest the butane from Hardis's lighter, crippling or killing the man.

Danny retrieved the blue and white boxes from where they'd fallen on the floor. He handed the blue one to Miles.

"I assume there's a safe place in this facility to lock this thing up?"

Miles shrugged.

"Ask the oracle, then, genius." Danny looked for Olcha in the display in his glasses. Where was she? "Olcha, what are you up to. I need you."

"I was having a look at the American torture program."

Danny narrowed his eyes. "Anyone in particular you plan on using that on, Olcha?"

"Yes," she said, "on MacArthur."

There was an audible scream through the overhead speakers as though they were echoing back the many voices of victims tortured in that very room.

"You feel that, MacArthur?" said Ye-Rin. "I modified the program so that you can feel everything Hardis feels as he dies. That," she said, "is for what you did to me when you separated me from Danny. Being turned off wasn't enough for what you did. You should suffer."

Danny wondered what MacArthur could have done to Olcha when he hacked her that merited such a vengeful response. Maybe she would tell him about it in time.

The scream died to a whimper as Hardis bled out. MacArthur expired with him. There would be no taking his body to Jeremy. Both Hardis and his program had been deleted.

Ye-Rin and Miles stood same as Danny, staring dumbly at the dead body of the American spy.

Finally, Danny directed his gaze at the white box held lightly in his hand as he decided what to do next.

Chapter 18

The rocket lifted off from its launch pad at the Next Wave hanger outside the city. Its engines roared to life, a mixture of blues and oranges and reds that mimicked the sunset over the Taedong River. Danny Kim watched it from the roof of the nondescript skyscraper that housed the headquarters for the American spy network in Pyongyang.

Overhead, the rocket arced onto its back as it soared into space, carrying humanity, like Atlas, into the stars.

"I've been looking at the records," Danny said quietly, reverently as the awe of the moment dictated. No matter how many times he saw a rocket climb into orbit, the same sense of wonder struck him deep in the gut.

He continued. "They're lifting payloads of weapons into the sky over our heads," he said, "weapons that can rain death on anyone anywhere on the planet."

Ye-Rin's elbow nuzzled his on the railway. They hadn't spoken much after Hardis had died. Danny wasn't sure what to say to her.

Miles, on the other hand, acted content to say nothing ever again unless directly spoken to. It seemed to be his natural state. He stood a few paces behind them on the roof. If he was uncomfortable being so close to his new boss, he didn't show it. Then again, the man never had a gram of social sense.

Danny addressed the mathematician, "Miles, I think it's time you went back to America. I'm going to outfit you with a new identity. The Chinese and the Russians and the rest of the planet will be looking for you once word gets out about what happened here."

"Okay, Danny," he said.

"Can Mal take care of that?"

Olcha, can you take care of that?" he asked Ye-Rin.

"Tell him yourself. I reinstated your permissions."

Danny smiled. "Olcha, how's your dive into the programs going?"

"Great, sir!" she laughed. "It's easy-peasey."

Danny couldn't believe that a Korean school-girl had taken charge of one of the most sophisticated computer network on the planet.

Danny spoke to Miles. "You'll have to hide. Do you have a name in mind?"

Miles stood still for a moment. The strong wind blowing against the roof of the tall building toyed with his wispy hair.

"The oracle," Miles said, "told me to choose the name Hawthorne Abendsen."

"That specific?"

"I'm to move to Wyoming."

"Well, Mal, you got that?"

"Sir, yes sir!" Ye-Rin's program replied.

Danny read the text scrolling across the display on his glasses. "Okay. Mal's got you booked for a flight out today. You've got access to a large bank account. Take nothing. Buy what you need in Wyoming."

"Cheyenne."

"Right, whatever. You know better than most what's coming."

"Yes. The oracle has shown me the future," said Miles. Yet he didn't move.

Danny looked at the top of Ye-Rin's head. He had to fight against the urge to kiss the place where her hair parted, flowing to the right and to the left and down the back over her shoulders.

"I know that I told you I'd buy you a new scooter," he said.

She slapped him playfully on the arm. "You took care of Jeremy. That's payment enough."

"He's going to pull through," Danny said. He had a second-by-second report streaming in from the hospital. "So is Sister Choi." Danny frowned. He was watching her too.

The Americans had their fingers in a lot of pies. Danny took turns tasting the data from each one.

"Olcha told me about Jeremy," said Ye-Rin. "She said that he had a backup of every vital organ. He got the idea from an old science fiction television show about a warrior race."

Danny hadn't exactly been surprised. The hints that Olcha dropped had prompted him to ask for the medic.

"So that's it then, everything wrapped up? No loose ends?" said Ye-Rin.

Danny shook his head.

"Are you sure this is what you want?" she asked.

"I want us to be together," he said.

"I'm not going to change," said Ye-Rin.

"I'm not either," said Danny.

Ye-Rin looked deeply into his eyes. "That's not what He told me."

"Who?"

"You know exactly who," she said, linking her elbow in his, she winked at him.

Great, thought Danny. Well, he said it would take an act of God to change him. According to Ye-Rin, God had been listening and had actually talked back. Danny would have laughed at anyone who told such a story; yet, he'd been there when it happened. He couldn't discount his own experience. But it was going to take a lot more convincing than the whisper of a disembodied spirit over the ether.

"If we're together in this," he said. "There's no going back."

"I know," said Ye-Rin.

Miles stood back watching the whole intimate show. Danny hoped the man would find a very understanding woman in Cheyenne. With the kind of money he'd been given, that shouldn't be too hard.

"Okay, then," said Danny. "I think we're done here."

He held his hand over the railing of the high tower. Unscrewing the lid, Danny opened the white box, pouring its invisible contents into the air.

They stood for a moment in silence. Miles turned and left.

He'd said he had to be there to see the mission through, thought Danny. And he had been.

"What do you think is going to happen?" said Ye-Rin.

Danny watched through his display as Olcha issued the agreed upon warnings to the major companies and countries of the world.

"We're going to return to a simpler existence," he said.

"I think you'd better buy me a horse instead of a scooter."

"There's still the steam engine," said Danny, "or the electric car."

Steampunk would become a real thing, thought Danny, which Jeremy would certainly appreciate. Danny had achieved Mfume Will's dream.

Ye-Rin looked up at the exhaust trail left by the rocket. "It's a shame about space though."

"We'll get there," said Danny, "eventually and without destroying the planet in the process."

"And what are you going to do without war and intrigue?" she asked, hugging against him for warmth on that breezy building.

"There will still be war," said Danny, "Except all that expensive equipment, jets, aircraft carriers, missiles, will have to be melted down for scrap. If someone so much as farts, the bugs will eat their lunch."

"You aren't serious," said Ye-Rin. "The methane, those poor cows."

"The cows and pigs will be fine. Nobody will explode from passing gas. Jeremy assured me the bugs only attack processed fuels."

"Danny," said Ye-Rin, adding a hint of seriousness to her voice, "you still didn't tell me what you're going to do once we're back in the stone age."

"Did I ever tell you that I'm descended from kings?"

She shook her head and smiled. "Don't all Koreans say that?"

"I'm thinking of taking up the family business," he said, "leading a truly unified Korea, free from all foreign meddling." Using the blackmail that the Americans had on every member of the Korean government, Danny thought that he just might be able to do it.

"Korea's never been free from foreign meddling," Ye-Rin elbowed him.

She knew her history, he had to admit.

"True enough," Danny smiled at the gentle ribbing. "But we Kim's have learned a thing or two over the past thirty-plus centuries. It's going to be a new, old world."

Ye-Rin sheltered under his arm as the sun finally set.

She was going to make a splendid queen.

"And what about me?" said Olcha. Ever the school-girl, she had to ruin the perfect moment. "You're lucky this drone can recharge on sunlight, or else you'd miss me all right!"

"Olcha," said Danny, "the only time I miss you is when you're silent."

"Fine!" Olcha retorted. She blew a raspberry, sounding as though she had a tongue poised directly over his ear. "Then I'll be quiet and make you suffer!"

Danny was perfectly all right with that. He went back to enjoying the moment with Ye-Rin.

Overhead, Olcha rode the drone into the sky. The silhouettes of the buildings against the orange sunset created a skyline that was recognizable around the world. The neon lights from Reunification Square bled into the growing dusk. The sounds of car horns and pedestrians drifted up from the streets below. Olcha beheld in all its glory, Pyongyang.

Thanks!

Thanks for reading the book. I hope you liked it. If you want to know more about Danny and Ye-Rin, please let me know. I rely on reader feedback to decide which stories get priority.

www.hanshergot.com

Also, please consider adding a review over at Amazon or Goodreads. Honest reviews really help independent authors connect to new readers.

Finally, please sign up for my mailing list:

tinyurl.com/hergotlist

About the Author

Hans Hergot is the penname of, well, me. I've lived in Korea for the better part of the last decade, and I enjoy writing science fiction and fantasy with a redemptive message. If you liked this book, you might also check out my book, *The Moondial*.

If you want to learn more about Korea, you might check out my other series for children, *Carrie Anne in Korea*, written under the name David Lee. It's about a time-travelling tween who explores Korea past and present.

The original Hans Hergot lived nearly five hundred years ago. He was a writer, a pamphleteer, and a book seller who wandered from village to village bringing knowledge and truth. He was burned alive for speaking a wisdom that the world could not understand.

Deo vindice